Published by

Smart Apple Media

123 South Broad Street

Mankato, Minnesota 56001

☼

Copyright © 2000 Smart Apple Media.

International copyrights reserved in all countries.

No part of this book may be reproduced in any form without

written permission from the publisher.

Printed in the United States of America.

—

Photos by George K. Peck,

Jeffrey Rich, Michele Warren, Joe McDonald/UNIPHOTO,

Richard Day, Rick Poley/Hillstrom Stock Photo, Inc.,

Bates Littlehales/Animals Animals

Editorial assistance by Barbara Ciletti

—

ISBN 1-887068-98-8

Library of Congress Catalog Card Number: 99-71161

First Edition 5 4 3 2 1

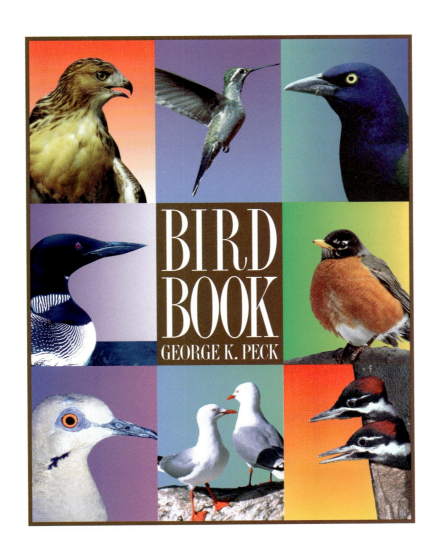

BIRD BOOK

GEORGE K. PECK

SMART APPLE MEDIA

C O N T E N T S

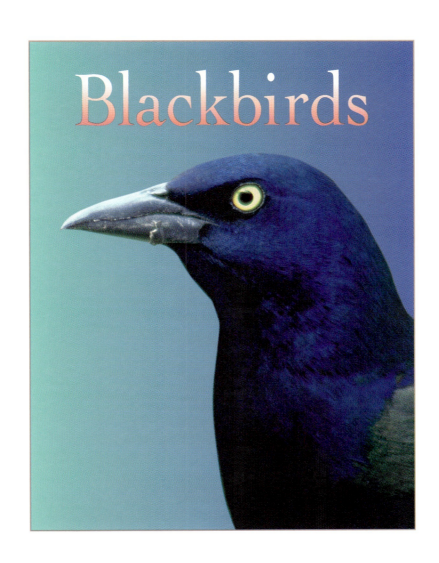

Blackbirds

Sing a song of sixpence,

a pocket full of rye;

four and

twenty blackbirds

baked in a pie.

Not all birds called "blackbirds" are true blackbirds.

The "blackbirds" in this Mother Goose rhyme were a type of thrush. In America, the birds we call blackbirds are members of the Icteridae family.

Not all members of the blackbird family are black.

The Icteridae family includes 97 different species of birds, from the yellow-breasted Meadowlark to the bright orange Northern Oriole. Of these 97 species, about 40 are mostly black in color. These are the birds we commonly call "blackbirds."

Not all black birds are blackbirds.

Just because a bird is black does not make it a member of the blackbird family. Two of the most common black-colored birds in North America—the crow and the starling—are not true blackbirds—no matter how black they look. You can't always judge a bird by its feathers!

The Icteridae family is native to the Americas. Most blackbirds prefer the tropics, but there are 11 species of blackbirds that live and breed in the United States and Canada. Because there are so many different kinds of blackbirds, this resourceful bird family can be found in a wide variety of habitats, from the northernmost forests of Canada to the steamy coasts of Florida and Texas. No matter where you live, you are sure to have a few blackbirds for neighbors.

The Red-winged Blackbird, our most common blackbird, is found throughout the United States and southern Canada. During the summer months, Red-winged Blackbirds are often found near freshwater marshes, lakes, and rivers. The Tricolored and Yellow-headed Blackbirds also live around fresh water. The Boat-tailed Grackle likes water too, but it prefers the saltwater marshes along the southeastern coast. The Common Grackle chooses to live in open woodlands and in cities, whereas the Rusty Blackbird makes its home far to the north, in Canada's cool evergreen forests.

The four species of blackbirds known as cowbirds avoid forested areas in North America. They are called cowbirds because they frequent open pastures—just like cattle! The Brown-headed Cowbird is a common sight on farms and ranches across the United States.

A Common Grackle perched in an evergreen in Ontario.

Some bird families are very specialized. Ducks and geese have bodies built for living and feeding on the water. Hawks have claws and sharp, hooked bills designed for capturing and devouring small animals—a hawk wouldn't know what to do with a sunflower seed! Hummingbirds' long beaks and tongues are made for sipping nectar from flower blossoms. Woodpeckers have special beaks and feet that allow them to walk up and down tree trunks, hammering holes in the wood when they hear a tasty insect hiding inside.

Blackbirds are not so specialized. They are multi-purpose birds that live in many places and eat many different things. You won't find any giant blackbirds the size of eagles, and there are no tiny blackbirds the size of hummingbirds. Most blackbirds are average in size—about the size of a robin. The smallest North American blackbird, the Brown-headed Cowbird, is 7 inches (18 cm) long. The Great-tailed Grackle is bigger—up to 18 inches (46 cm) long—but half of its length is its tail!

In general, blackbirds have long, pointed wings. Their legs are made for walking instead of hopping, and they have sharp, cone-shaped beaks. The blackbird beak is a multi-purpose tool. It can shell a sunflower seed, snatch a buzzing fly from the air, spear an unlucky beetle, or—in the case of the Great-tailed Grackle—crack open an acorn.

Most blackbirds look mostly black.

But a closer look shows some surprising colors. The male Tricolored Blackbird has a bright red-and-white patch on each wing. The Red-winged Blackbird has a red-and-yellow patch. The male Yellow-headed Blackbird shows off a head and chest of brilliant gold. The females of these species tend to be less colorful. The female Red-winged Blackbird is a smaller brown-and-cream striped bird. If you don't look closely, you might mistake it for a large sparrow.

On a cloudy day, male grackles appear to be solid black, but when the sunlight strikes their feathers, they shine blue, bronze, and purple! This type of reflected color is called iridescence. You can see the same effect when you look at a sheen of oil floating on water. Common Grackles and Great-tailed Grackles also have bright yellow eyes, making them quite colorful for a "black" bird!

Female grackles look much like the males, but their iridescence is not as noticeable and they are smaller—the female Great-tailed Grackle is only two-thirds the size of the male.

The Brewer's Blackbird looks a lot like a grackle, but it is smaller and has a shorter, thicker bill. The males have yellow eyes and iridescent feathers, and the females are a duller blackish-brown color. Its close relative, the Rusty Blackbird, is the same size and shape, but it has rust-colored tips on its black feathers in fall plumage.

The male Brown-headed Cowbird has a blue-black sheen to its small body and, as its name indicates, a brown head. The female is gray-brown across its back and tail, with a paler breast area. The Bronzed Cowbird, a species found in Texas, Arizona, and Mexico, has similar coloring but is slightly larger and has a longer bill.

Swallows eat only insects. Hummingbirds live mostly on flower nectar. The pelican's diet is fish and more fish. Finches and cardinals want almost nothing but seeds.

Blackbirds are not so fussy. Blackbirds will eat insects, grain, fruit, or just about anything else that looks like food and is small enough for them to swallow.

Grackles are the least particular of all. They will dine on everything from frogs to acorns to other birds' eggs. They are notorious thieves, and are attracted to parks and picnic grounds where there is plenty of food to be found. You might even see a grackle fly off with a whole hamburger bun in its beak!

Cowbirds prefer insects for dinner, although they will not refuse a bird feeder full of seed. Red-winged Blackbirds are very fond of rice, wheat, and other grains. As many an angry farmer will tell you, a flock of Red-wings can eat up a lot of grain!

Brewer's Blackbird eating a minnow in Yellowstone.

Blackbirds are strong fliers, able to travel at more than 30 miles per hour (48 kph). Red-winged Blackbirds have a wave-like, up-and-down flight pattern. Grackles fly in a straight line, using their long tails as rudders.

In the spring and fall, blackbirds gather in flocks to migrate. In the fall, before the snow falls in the north, they fly south to avoid the cold winter winds. Some species travel as far south as Central America. In the spring, they fly north to their breeding grounds. Rusty Blackbirds fly as far north as the Arctic Circle to breed.

In the winter, Red-winged Blackbirds form huge flocks. They like to be around other blackbirds. Sometimes they are joined by grackles and cowbirds. One winter flock of blackbirds in Virginia contained 15 million birds—so many birds that when they took off the sky turned black. That would make a lot of blackbird pies!

Once the blackbirds return to their northern breeding grounds in the spring, they quickly establish nesting territories and choose their mates.

In late February or early March, the male Red-winged Blackbirds arrive, a few days before the females. They choose their territories, usually in wetland areas or shrubby pastures. The males sit atop the highest cattails or shrubs. With a shrill *o-ka-leee*, they announce to one and all that they have claimed an area as their own. Any other male blackbird had better stay away—the Red-winged Blackbird will defend its territory with its sharp beak and claws.

When the female Red-winged Blackbirds arrive, they must choose a mate. The male performs a courtship display. He spreads his wings and tail and raises his body feathers to make himself look bigger. He erects his bright red shoulder feathers, singing *o-ka-leee* over and over again. If the female likes what she sees, she might do a little dance of her own! If the females outnumber the males, some males might end up with more than one mate.

Every blackbird species has its own courtship display. Although blackbirds are not known for having beautiful voices, the males give it everything they've got during courtship. Their calls range from the Brown-headed Cowbird's squeaky gurgling to the creaky cry of the Common Grackle. The Great-tailed Grackle's "song" is a loud, piercing *may-reee,* and a high-pitched squeal: *quee-ee, quee-ee!*

Of course, the male blackbirds don't care what humans think of their songs. They just want to keep other males away.

Once the females choose their mates, nest building begins.

The female Red-winged Blackbird builds a nest on the upright stalks of dead cattails or tall grasses. She uses coarse grass and strips of cattail leaves, then lines the inside of the cup-shaped nest with fine, soft grass to protect her eggs. Most Red-winged Blackbird nests are only a foot or two above the ground.

Grackles and Rusty Blackbirds prefer to build their nests in evergreen trees. Their nests are made from sticks and twigs, with softer grasses lining the inside. Boat-tailed Grackles look for a tree with a view—their nest can be as high as 80 feet (24 m) above the ground.

Cowbirds are one of the few birds that do not make a nest at all. Cowbirds are a traveling species. It has been theorized that for hundreds of thousands of years, cowbirds followed the bison herds across the American prairie, feeding on insects that were stirred up by the thundering herds. Because they were always on the move, the cowbirds lost their nest-building skills. Instead, they began to lay their eggs in other birds' nests and leave them there for the other birds to raise. Birds that use other birds to raise their young are called brood parasites.

Cowbirds are not particular about whose nest they invade—robins, warblers, sparrows, or other blackbirds—it's all the same to the cowbird. They usually lay only one egg per nest, but a single female cowbird may lay dozens of eggs in a year—each one in a different nest. The Brown-headed Cowbird has been known to parasitize 220 different bird species. It is important for cowbirds to spread their eggs around because some host birds will not accept a cowbird egg. Robins, Eastern Kingbirds, and Cedar Waxwings will roll the cowbird egg out onto the ground. The Yellow Warbler simply builds a new nest right on top of the old one, then lays a new clutch of eggs. But many other species—such as the Red-winged Blackbird—don't seem to notice that they have acquired a strange egg.

Most North American blackbirds lay clutches of two to seven eggs. The female Red-winged Blackbird lays one egg per day until she has a clutch of two to six eggs. The exact number of eggs depends on the age and health of the mother and the amount of food available. Red-winged Blackbird eggs are a beautiful pale blue-green, with black, brown, and purple speckles and streaks around the large end.

After the eggs are laid, the mother blackbird sits on her nest, keeping the eggs warm and safe by covering them with her body. This is called incubation and it helps the baby blackbirds grow inside their eggs.

In 11 to 14 days, the baby blackbirds peck their way out of the shells. Their eyes are closed and their bodies are covered only with a bit of fluffy gray down. A baby blackbird knows how to do just one thing: open its mouth for food! For the next two weeks, the mother blackbird is kept very busy. She brings them insects, spiders, and even snails. The babies never seem to get enough to eat. They eat their own weight in food every day. Sometimes the male blackbird helps feed the babies if he has only one mate.

Red-winged Blackbird babies grow quickly on their rich diet. By the third day, hard cases called feather sheaths appear on the baby blackbird's body. Inside these sheaths, tiny soft feathers are growing. By the end of the first week, the babies' feathers have come out of the sheaths. Around the tenth day, baby Red-winged Blackbirds have most of their feathers. Since the babies are much larger now, they hop out of the nest and perch nearby. They still cannot fly or feed themselves, and the mother is more busy than ever finding enough food for her family.

All blackbird babies are able to fly by the time they are three weeks old. Young Red-winged Blackbirds quickly venture off on their own, and their parents may set out to raise a second family. Common Grackles do not get rid of their young so easily. Baby grackles will follow their parents around for weeks begging food.

Cowbird babies tend to dominate their host nests. They usually hatch sooner and grow more quickly than the other babies. They get most of the food, and the other babies often die from starvation. But sometimes the situation is reversed: if a cowbird egg hatches in the nest of an American Goldfinch or some other seed-eating bird, it will not survive. The goldfinch feeds its young seeds, not insects. In this case, it is the baby cowbird who will starve!

During the first summer, young blackbirds—both male and female—look like small, plump versions of their mothers. By September, they have molted, or shed, their juvenal feathers. The new feathers make them look more like their parents, with the males showing the glossy black or colored feathers of the adult. By the following spring they are full-grown adult birds, ready to raise families on their own.

D A N G E R S

A blackbird can live for as long as 18 years. But the average blackbird will survive only two or three years in the wild. Like all wild creatures, blackbirds face many dangers. Many die before they ever leave their nests, killed by wind or rain, or by a hungry snake, raccoon, or even another blackbird! Some birds are killed by storms during migration. Even on a beautiful, cloudless day, an adult blackbird risks its life. It could be struck by a car, or fly into a window, or be snatched in midflight by a Sharp-shinned Hawk. For a bird that weighs only a few ounces, the world is a dangerous place.

To a blackbird, the most dangerous creature of all is the human being. When a farmer sees a cloud of thousands of blackbirds landing in his fields, he worries that all his hard work will be gobbled up. Many blackbirds are trapped, shot, or poisoned by humans trying to protect their crops. Some grain might be saved by killing birds, but most of the blackbirds' diet is insects, including corn borers and other crop pests. If it wasn't for blackbirds, we might lose more of our crops to insect invasions. Also, much of the grain eaten by blackbirds is waste seed left behind after the harvest. In the long run, blackbirds might be doing us more good than harm.

Blackbirds are also in danger from new construction in wetland areas. Red-winged, Yellow-headed, and Tricolored Blackbirds depend on wetlands for food and breeding space. When people invade these areas, draining swamps and spraying pesticides to kill mosquitoes, they are taking away the blackbirds' food and shelter.

With their noisy calls and large appetites, blackbirds are not always appreciated by people. But they remain an important part of our natural world. Even the Brown-headed Cowbird, with its parasitic ways, fills an important niche in our ecosystem.

The world would be a poorer place without the wheeling flocks of blackbirds filling the sky each spring and fall, the glossy, iridescent grackle doing his courtship dance, or the joyful sight of a Red-winged Blackbird, singing *o-ka-leee*, perched proudly at the tip of a waving cattail.

Doves

For thousands

of years the dove

has symbolized

hope and peace.

In the Bible story of Noah's Ark, the earth was covered by a great flood. Only Noah and the animals on his ark survived. The ark came to rest atop a mountain. Noah sent forth a dove to search for dry land. When the dove returned, Noah knew that it was safe to leave the ark.

For the dove carried a green olive branch in its bill.

The dove described in the story of Noah could have been the bird we now call the Rock Dove, also known as the Common Pigeon. It is one of our oldest domesticated animals. More than 4,000 years ago, Rock Doves were raised in Egypt for food. They were also used to carry important messages long distances. Julius Caesar used them to send news of his victories back to Rome. Until the invention of the telegraph, domesticated Rock Doves were the fastest way to communicate over long distances!

There are more than 300 species of wild doves and pigeons in the Columbidae family. The larger members of the family are usually called pigeons and the smaller species are commonly called doves, but there is no scientific distinction between them. Sometimes the two words are used for the same bird, as in the case of the Rock Dove, better known as the Common Pigeon.

Doves and pigeons live all over the world, except in the colder polar regions. They are common in the biggest cities, in open deserts, and in dense forests. Some species live mostly in trees, while others spend most of their time on the ground. They may be sociable birds, living in groups, or solitary. Some, such as the Mourning Dove, are sociable during part of the year and solitary at other times.

Eight native dove and pigeon species now live and breed in the United States and Canada. Four other species—the Rock Dove, the Eurasian Collared-Dove, the Ringed Turtle Dove, and the Spotted Dove—were originally brought to North America by settlers and now live and breed in the wild. The Rock Dove is one of the best known birds of our cities and towns. The other non-native species also live near people, where food is plentiful and they can nest on buildings and other man-made structures.

Our best known native dove, the Mourning Dove, is found in a wide variety of habitats throughout southern Canada and the continental United States. The White-winged Dove lives in the desert regions of the southwestern

United States. The Band-tailed Pigeon can be found in oak and pine forests in the West.

The Passenger Pigeon, a native species that was once the most numerous bird in North America, is now extinct. Passenger Pigeons once lived throughout the deciduous forests of eastern North America, feeding on acorns, beechnuts, and chestnuts. In the 1800s, most of the eastern forests were cleared to farm the land. Loss of habitat and overhunting eventually caused the Passenger Pigeons to die off.

Doves vary greatly in size. Australia's Diamond Dove is only 7 1/2 inches (19 cm) in length, including its long tail. The Plain-breasted Ground-Dove of Central America has a slightly larger body, but because it has a short tail, it is less than 6 inches (15.3 cm) long. Both of these tiny doves are about the size of the common House Sparrow.

The largest living dove is the Blue-crowned Pigeon of New Guinea. It measures 33 inches (84 cm) long, about the size of a small turkey.

An early relative of the dove family, the flightless Dodo, once lived on the island of Mauritius in the Indian Ocean. An adult Dodo weighed as much as 50 pounds (23 kg)! Dodos have been extinct since 1681.

Most doves have small heads, plump bodies, and thick, fleshy legs. Their feet have short, curved claws and are adapted for both walking and perching. Legs and feet are usually pink or reddish. They have straight bills, slightly downturned at the tip, with a fleshy area at the base called a cere. Bills can be yellow, pink, red, black, or a combination of these colors.

Ground-dwelling doves have short, rounded wings. Other species have longer, pointed wings. The Mourning Dove has a long, pointed tail. The Common Ground-Dove's tail is short and fan-shaped.

Domestic pigeon varieties, descended from the wild Rock Dove, may have very different body shapes. The White King is raised, like chickens and turkeys, for food. It is a short, stocky, broad-breasted bird with pure white plumage. The "pouter" pigeon has long legs and a puffed-out chest. The "fantail" pigeon has a large, fan-shaped tail, and the "fairy swallow" has feet covered by long feathers.

Doves and pigeons have soft, thick feathers that easily pull out of the skin. The most common colors are pale shades of brown, gray, and pink, but some species, such as the Pink-necked Green-Pigeon of New Guinea, are among the most colorful of birds.

Males and females of most species are difficult to tell apart. The male and female Mourning Dove look nearly identical with grayish-brown backs and wings and a pinkish wash on their undersides. The Spotted Dove has a distinctive white-spotted black collar around the back of its neck. The White-winged Dove, a native southwestern species, looks a lot like the Mourning Dove, but it has white bands on its wings and a shorter, rounded tail.

Ground doves are some of our best camouflaged birds. When they are feeding or nesting on the ground, their mottled gray and brown feathers make them almost invisible.

Some of the most beautiful and unusual colorations are found on the common pigeons that inhabit our parks and city streets. If you look at a typical group of city pigeons you will see an amazing variety of colors, from pure white to shades of brown, rust, pink, green, and gold.

Common city pigeons are descended from the wild Rock Dove. The Rock Dove, the ancestor of all domestic pigeons, has slate gray plumage, a white rump, two black bars on the wings, a black band on the tip of the tail, and iridescent green and purple feathers on the neck.

A Rock Dove in Ontario.

Ground-feeding doves eat a variety of seeds and grains. Some doves also eat grasses, leaves, insects, and snails. The Band-tailed Pigeon feeds on fruits and berries. In the Southwest, the White-winged Dove eats cactus fruit in addition to seeds and grains.

Doves will eat many different foods, depending on what is available. In the wild, the Rock Dove feeds mostly on seeds and grains. But Rock Doves that live in our cities are happy eating bits of bread, popcorn, and cookies.

When hard seeds and grains are part of their diet, doves will also swallow small bits of gravel and sand. This grit is stored in a muscular part of the stomach called the gizzard. The grit helps the gizzard grind up the hard seeds, making them easier to digest.

Have you ever watched a bird drink? Most birds drink by dipping their bills into the water, getting a mouthful, then raising their heads to swallow. They do this again and again until they aren't thirsty anymore. Doves drink differently from other birds. They dip their bills in just once and suck up water until their thirst is satisfied.

A White-tipped Dove feeding in Texas.

Most doves are strong flyers, but the champion of the family is the Homing Pigeon, a domesticated breed of Rock Dove. One of the swiftest of all birds, the "homer" can fly 82 miles per hour (132 kph). The Homing Pigeon was originally bred to carry messages home. Wherever it is released, it has the amazing ability to find its way back to its home loft. In the sport of pigeon racing, "homers" are taken many miles from their home loft and released to see how fast they can find their way back.

One pigeon owned by the Duke of Wellington was released in southwest Africa and found its way back to England, 5,700 miles (9,170 km) away. Unfortunately for the bird, it was found dead just one mile from its home loft.

Passenger Pigeons were also swift flyers—estimated to reach speeds of 70 miles per hour (112 kph)—but not swift enough to escape the shotguns of hunters. The Mourning Dove can fly at speeds of 55 miles per hour (88 kph). Even the Common Ground-Dove, with its short wings and small body, can reach speeds of 32 miles per hour (51 kph).

If doves are startled or take flight suddenly, they will sometimes clap their wings together over their backs. Wing clapping is also performed by male doves during courtship.

In the fall, some North American dove species migrate south in search of warmer weather and more plentiful food. The Mourning Dove may travel only a few hundred miles. The western Band-tailed Pigeon migrates from

British Columbia, Washington, and Oregon down into California and Mexico.

The Rock Dove, an urban dweller, does not migrate at all, even though it is capable of flying long distances quickly. Southern species such as the Common Ground-Dove and the Inca Dove also stay in the same areas.

If you live in a city, you have probably heard the *coo-a-roo* of the Rock Dove, or Common Pigeon. The sad-sounding *coah, cooo, cooo, coo* of the Mourning Dove is often heard in our backyards and gardens. Other dove species have their distinctive "coos" too.

The doves' cooing is most often heard in the spring when the male dove coos to attract female doves and to warn other males away from his territory. The courting male will also "show off" to the female by bowing, spreading his tail, bobbing his head, and strutting. Rock Doves will often turn in complete circles, performing a kind of dance for the female. Courtship might also include repeated wing clapping while in flight, and the males often peck at the females at the beginning of their courtship. Fights between males can be ferocious.

A more gentle part of courtship is called "billing." The male opens his bill and the female puts her bill into his mouth. In some species, the male feeds the female.

After courtship, the pair mate and a nest site is selected, usually by the male. The area near the nest is defended by both the male and the female. Some dove species, such as the Mourning Dove, usually nest alone. Others nest in colonies. The Passenger Pigeon nested in huge colonies. One Passenger Pigeon colony in Wisconsin covered 850 square miles (2210 km^2) of forest and contained 136 million birds!

Doves nest in a variety of places. The wild Rock Dove nests in caves or crevices on cliffs. Its city relatives nest on ledges, beams, rafters, and other parts of buildings and bridges. The Common Ground-Dove often nests on the ground. Some dove species nest in tree cavities or use the abandoned nests of other birds. The Mourning Dove builds a twiggy nest in trees or shrubs. In desert areas, they will even nest in prickly cactus plants or on the ground.

Once the nest site has been chosen and the nest built, the female lays one or two eggs. The eggs are usually pure white, though some doves lay cream- or coffee-colored eggs.

Rock Doves may nest at any time of the year, raising several broods of young doves. Mourning Doves nest from March through October and can raise up to three broods a year.

The eggs must stay warm to help the baby doves inside them grow. Both the male and female doves take turns sitting on the eggs. The male usually sits on the eggs during the day, the female at night. Before the eggs are laid, the adult birds get a brood patch, or a bare patch of warm skin on their bellies. The heat from the warm patch of skin helps the baby doves grow quickly. The eggs hatch in 14 to 15 days.

The eggs and nest of a White-winged Dove in Texas.

While they are still inside their eggs, baby doves grow a hard bump called an egg tooth on their bills. Most baby birds have an egg tooth. Without it, they wouldn't be able to break out of their shells.

Inside the egg, the baby dove pecks a circle at the large end of the shell, breaking it open. After the baby dove has hatched, the egg tooth falls off.

Doves are born helpless, with their eyes closed and only a slight covering of soft down. For the first few days, the baby doves are fed pigeon's milk, a thick, nutritious liquid made in their parents' crops. The crop is a pouch inside the bird's neck where food is stored. Both parents feed the babies, bringing pigeon's milk up from their crops into their mouths. The babies take the food right out of the parent's mouth.

As the babies grow older, the parents will add small insects and seeds to the babies' diet. They will continue to give the babies pigeon's milk until they are able to fly.

In a few days, stiff quills grow to replace the down. Feathers soon sprout from the quills. Within two weeks, the young birds are fully feathered and ready to fly. In another week, they will be on their own.

Like all wild animals, doves face many dangers. About 70 percent of young doves will die in their first year. Eggs and nestlings can be destroyed by high winds. Many adult doves are killed by flying into TV antennas and utility wires.

Predators are a constant threat. Squirrels, raccoons, and snakes will raid nests and eat both eggs and young doves. Doves are a favorite food source for hawks and falcons.

The Peregrine Falcon, one of the world's swiftest birds, hunts doves every chance it gets. Peregrine Falcons now live in many cities, nesting on tall buildings and hunting for Rock Doves. When chased by a falcon, the Rock Dove will swoop around and between buildings and trees at tremendous speeds, swerving down and sideways and diving, in full flight, into any hole it sees.

In captivity a Mourning Dove can live as long as 17 years. Domesticated pigeons might live for 6 to 16 years. In the wild, it is possible for a Mourning Dove to live 10 years or longer, but few survive that long.

The dove's greatest enemy is the human hunter. In the 1800s, Passenger Pigeons were hunted to extinction. Fortunately, dove hunting is now regulated.

Hunting and loss of habitat, however, do threaten many other dove species. The Puerto Rican Plain Pigeon, the Mauritius Pink Pigeon, the Seychelles Turtle-Dove, and the Victoria Crowned-Pigeon of New Guinea are now endangered. Some species are extremely rare and are on the verge of extinction.

Doves and humans have had a close relationship for thousands of years. The Rock Dove, our oldest domesticated species, is still used for food, for the sport of pigeon racing, and for show. Rock Doves and Mourning Doves have adapted to humans and are some of the most common wild animals living in our towns and cities, but other species have suffered from human contact.

The extinction of the Passenger Pigeon is one of the most tragic examples of how humans can destroy a species. Two hundred years ago there were between three and five billion Passenger Pigeons in North America—more than a quarter of all the birds on the continent! In less than 100 years, overhunting and land clearing reduced their numbers to a few million, and then a few thousand. The last wild Passenger Pigeon was shot in Ohio in 1900. The last Passenger Pigeon on our planet died in a Cincinnati zoo on September 1, 1914.

Gulls

In Salt Lake City, Utah, there stands a tall bronze monument to a savior of the Mormon people. But the statue is not of a soldier, a saint, or a politician. It is a statue of a California Gull.

In the summer of 1848, shortly after the Mormons settled the Salt Lake Valley, millions of Mormon Crickets began to devour the crops. Things looked bad for the settlers. Without their corn and wheat crops, they might not survive the coming winter.

Then the gulls came.

Thousands upon thousands of hungry California Gulls swept into the valley, eating their fill of crickets. Most of the damage had been done, but some of the crops were saved. When winter came, the Mormons had just enough food to survive. A statue was built to honor the California gull.

Today, the California Gull is the state bird of Utah.

Gulls are part of a large group of waterbirds that are found on and near oceans, lakes, and rivers. Wherever open water appears on the surface of our planet, you are likely to find gulls or their close relatives, the terns. Auks, skimmers, skuas, jaegers, and many small shorebirds such as sandpipers and plovers are also related to gulls. There are 51 species of gulls in our world. Eighteen species are known to live and breed in the United States and Canada.

Because gulls are so common in coastal areas, they are often called "sea gulls," but gulls are also found inland on lakes, rivers, and ponds.

The Franklin's Gull breeds in the prairie marshes of Alberta, Saskatchewan, and Manitoba. In the winter, it migrates to coastal areas of Central and South America. Bonaparte's Gull prefers ponds in the northern forests of Alaska and Canada, and it winters on both the Atlantic and Pacific coasts and on the Great Lakes.

Iceland Gulls gather in colonies on island cliff ledges in the far north, like those of Iceland, Greenland, and Baffin Island. They winter in North America along the Atlantic coast from Newfoundland all the way down to Virginia. The most northern species of all is the Ivory Gull, a pure white gull that is rarely seen below the Arctic Circle—not even during the winter! Colonies of Ivory Gulls nest on the northernmost islands, where snow and ice stay on the ground all year long.

The Herring Gull, one of North America's most common gulls, nests singly and in colonies all across Canada and the northern United States. It also nests on the Atlantic coast down to South Carolina, near both freshwater and saltwater. The equally common Ring-billed Gull nests in large colonies on islands and the shores of freshwater lakes and rivers, from Newfoundland in the east to Washington and Oregon in the west. Ring-billed Gulls spend their winters in the southern United States and Mexico.

Wherever there is open water, you will find gulls. They avoid only the driest, hottest deserts and the coldest parts of the Polar regions.

Gulls vary in size from the Great Black-backed Gull (about the size of a small goose), to the Little Gull (about the size of a pigeon), but all have some features in common.

Gulls are scavengers. They eat what they can find, wherever they find it, and their bodies are perfectly adapted to their lifestyle. They spend much of their time in the air, scanning the shoreline for a dead fish, a scrap of bread, or anything else that looks tasty. Their long narrow wings are perfect for spending long hours in the air. And when a gull does find food, its long bill with its hooked tip is strong and sharp enough to tear into almost anything—whether it be slippery, flopping fish, or a stolen bag of potato chips!

When gulls are not flying, they are either walking or swimming, and their long legs and webbed toes are built to do both. Dense, compact feathers keep gulls warm and dry, even when they are swimming in the coldest water.

The gull's ability to adapt to different environments and diets has made it one of the most successful and widespread bird families. They are one of the few warm-blooded animals able to drink both salt and fresh water. A pair of glands above their eyes helps get rid of the extra salt in their bodies.

Most adult gulls have gray backs and white undersides, and yellow, red, or black bills. Gull legs and feet are often yellow, but can also be red, pink, or black. Some species, like the Herring Gull and the Ring-billed Gull, can be hard to tell apart, but if you look closely, you can see a ring of black around the bill of the adult Ring-billed Gull. The adult Herring Gull has a small red spot on the bottom of its yellow bill.

Several gull species, such as the Great Black-backed Gull, have backs that are black or very dark gray. Some smaller species have black heads. The Ivory Gull of the far north is pure white. Heerman's Gull, which is found along the Pacific coast, is dark gray with a white head and a red bill.

Young gulls can be difficult to identify. Most one- and two-year-old gulls do not look like their parents. They are a mix of neutral shades of light, medium, and dark brown. Smaller gulls come into their adult plumage in their second year, but the bigger Herring Gull takes four years to become an adult—every year it looks different!

Even experts have trouble identifying young gulls—sometimes, you just have to wait for them to grow up.

Gulls eat just about anything. They clean up dead fish, crabs, and clams from harbors and beaches. They also eat live fish and prey on the eggs and young of other birds. Instead of diving deep underwater for food the way loons and penguins do, a gull will pick its catch off the water's surface.

In farming areas, flocks of gulls will follow the plows, feeding on the earthworms, grasshoppers, and other creatures disturbed by the plow blades.

Gulls also like people food, and will often gather near restaurants, picnic areas, and dumps. Almost anything will do—meat scraps, bread crusts, french fries, and chicken bones—for gulls, "junk food" is the best! The small gulls known as Black- and Red-legged Kittiwakes will follow ships far out to sea, waiting for food to be thrown overboard.

Some gulls can be very aggressive when it comes to eating. They steal food from other birds, especially the slow-moving Brown Pelican. Gulls steal from each other too. They will even snatch a treat from your picnic table.

Many beaches have signs that say, "Don't feed the gulls." This is because once you start feeding the gulls, the gulls won't leave you alone! Imagine being followed all day long by dozens of screeching, hungry birds!

In the fall, some gull species leave their northern breeding areas and head for warmer waters. Gulls that breed in northern inland areas must travel south, or to the ocean, where the water will not freeze.

Most gulls don't go any farther than they have to. The Ivory Gull stays at the edge of the Arctic ice pack. The Herring Gull flies to the nearest open water. Many coastal gulls remain in the same area all year long. The Franklin's Gull is one of the few gulls that migrates long distances—from Canada all the way to the tip of South America.

Gulls are strong, slow flyers with an average flight speed of 25 miles per hour (40 kph), but they can soar for days at a time, setting their long, narrow wings and letting the wind do the work. Gulls often face into the wind and simply hover as if by magic, looking down at the ocean surface and waiting for dinner to appear.

Laughing Gulls in flight on the coast of Padre Island, Texas.

Gulls live together in groups, or flocks. Most gulls also nest together in large groups called colonies. A few species, such as Bonaparte's and Sabine's Gulls, sometimes nest alone.

In North America, gulls arrive at their breeding grounds in the spring, after the snows have thawed. Breeding grounds are often islands or protected shorelines where the birds will not be disturbed. Kittiwakes and Iceland Gulls nest on high sea cliffs.

Tens of thousands of gulls might share a breeding territory, sometimes sharing it with other bird species such as pelicans, herons, and terns.

Gulls begin to court one another right after arrival. Both the male and female strut back and forth, making loud mewling and yodeling sounds—*ke-yow, ke-yow, ke-yow*! With thousands of gulls all calling and strutting about, trying to get one another's attention, the noise is incredible! Fights break out between competing males. Often, the male gull will offer the female food.

Somehow, in all the confusion, the gulls work things out. Mates from previous years find one another. Young males and females form new pairs. Once a bond is formed, a pair of gulls will often remain mates for life. They may go their separate ways in the winter, but each spring they will find one another and raise a new family.

The female gull chooses the nest site. In crowded colonies, the nests might be so close to each other that you would have trouble walking through them without stepping on one! If you did that, the gulls would create quite a ruckus. Gulls are very aggressive about defending their nests.

Most gulls place their nests on the bare ground, in grasses, on rocks, or on cliff ledges. Nests are usually mounds of grasses, weeds, sticks, or mosses. They may be lined with feathers.

Not all gulls nest on the ground. The Bonaparte's Gull builds its nest on a branch of a spruce tree. The Laughing and Little Gulls nest in marshes on floating mats of dead reeds. The Black-legged Kittiwake builds its cup-shaped nest on the narrow ledges of high cliffs. It is made of seaweed, grass, moss, and mud.

Females usually lay three eggs. Kittiwakes and the Ivory Gull usually lay only two. Some gull nests have been found with five or more eggs, but this is usually because more than one female gull has laid eggs in it. Gull eggs are often brown or gray with spots and splotches of darker gray, brown, or black. Franklin's Gull lays eggs of olive green, with dark brown spots. The mother Herring Gull lays eggs that are sometimes bluish and sometimes somewhat green or buff, speckled with brown.

After the eggs are laid, the parents take turns incubating them. The eggs must be kept warm so that the embryos can develop, and they must be protected from predators, including other gulls.

The babies hatch from their eggs after three to four weeks of incubation. The smaller Franklin's Gull comes out of its shell just after three weeks, whereas California Gull babies don't hatch for nearly a month. Gull babies come into the world covered with soft down, their eyes already open. In a colony, most of the baby gulls hatch within a few days of one another. Since hungry baby gulls demand constant attention, it's an exciting time in the colony!

Baby gulls are fed and protected by both parents. The adult gulls store food in their crops, which are pouches located in their throats. The young Herring Gulls peck at the red dot on their parents' bills. This is a signal for the adult gull to bring up some partially digested food from its crop. Several other gull species have similar red dots on their bills.

In a colony with thousands of nests that all look the same, you might wonder how a parent gull can find its own nest. Gulls' colonies do not have street names. They don't have numbers on their nests. Gull parents find their own young by listening for their cries. Every baby has a voice all its own. When it cries out, its parent knows who it is.

Young Herring Gulls leave the nest within two or three days, but they don't wander far. For several weeks they depend on their parents to bring them food. It takes five or six weeks for their flight feathers to grow. Until then, the young gulls remain near the nest. If a colony is disturbed, the young gulls will run to the water and swim until the danger has passed. Kittiwakes are born on the narrow ledges of high sea cliffs. Once they jump off that ledge, there will be no second chance, so young kittiwakes stay in their nests until they are ready to fly.

Once young gulls can fly, they learn to feed themselves. They continue to beg for food from their parents, but after a while they are on their own.

As summer turns to fall, the young birds go off on their own or with other young gulls their own age. Many won't be full adults until they're three or four years old. When they're all grown up, they return to the breeding grounds where they hatched. Here, they'll find mates and raise families of their own. They may breed at this same colony for the rest of their lives.

Gulls face many dangers at their nesting colonies. The eggs and young gulls are eaten by many different predators including foxes, raccoons, hawks, and owls. Skuas and jaegers, close relatives of the gulls, also take many eggs and young. In mixed colonies, even other gulls will steal eggs and young from unprotected nests.

About half of all gull chicks die before their first birthday. Not many gulls live to be more than ten years old, but one captive Herring is known to have lived to the ripe old age of 49.

Human beings sometimes disturb gulls by visiting their nesting sites. The gulls are upset by people walking near their nests. They may refuse to take care of their eggs or their babies once a colony has been invaded by human visitors. Human pollution also kills many gulls. Oil spills can completely destroy nesting colonies. Poisons in our lakes, rivers, and oceans eventually find their way into the stomachs of gulls and other waterbirds.

Some people don't like gulls.

They think gulls are noisy and aggressive and messy.

But imagine the seashore without the gulls. What do you see?

A silent beach covered with dead fish and garbage.

Gulls are terrific scavengers. They are partly responsible for keeping our beaches and oceans clean. And for those of us who take the time to watch their soaring flight and their unique behaviors, they are one of the most fascinating bird groups. From the common Herring Gull, to the ghostly Ivory Gull of the far north, they all play a part in this natural world we all share.

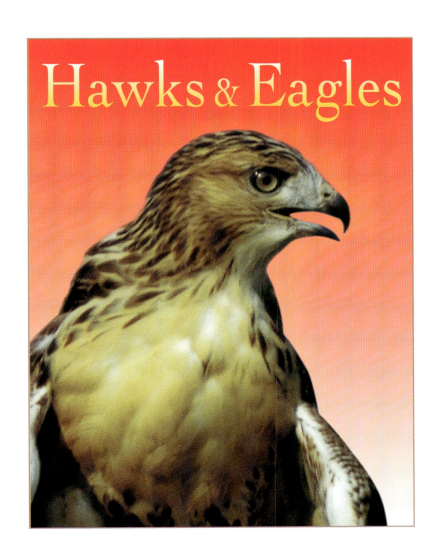

Hawks & Eagles

W hen the founding fathers of the United States searched for an animal symbol to represent their new nation, they looked at many powerful and admirable beasts.

The animal they chose would become the national emblem of the United States of America. They had to choose carefully.

There was the majestic bison, master of the Great Plains. The ferocious Grizzly Bear, the country's largest predator. The proud American Elk with its colossal antlers. Even the deadly Diamondback Rattlesnake and the spectacularly feathered Wild Turkey were considered.

They wanted an animal as wild and as strong as their new country. A creature both fierce and independent. Both powerful and beautiful. A creature to inspire admiration, awe, and reverence.

They chose the Bald Eagle.

Eagles and hawks belong to the family Accipitridae, which also includes kites, harriers, and ospreys. There are 224 species in the Accipitridae family, all of them birds of prey, or raptors. They live on every continent except Antarctica and are found in a wide variety of habitats, from dry desert regions to towering mountains, from the steamy tropics to the chilly Arctic tundra. Twenty-five species are known to live and breed in the United States and Canada.

Hawks and eagles have learned to survive in nearly every habitat. The Rough-legged Hawk breeds in the Arctic tundra, while the Harris' Hawk prefers the hot southwestern deserts. The Snail Kite is found in Florida's hot, humid Everglades. The Northern Harrier lives and hunts in open fields. The fast-flying Sharp-shinned and Cooper's Hawks live in forested areas where their speed and agility help them capture woodland birds in midflight.

Bald Eagles are found across most of North America. The Bald Eagle is a fish-eating member of the Accipitridae family and is usually seen near open water. Its close relative, the Golden Eagle, prefers mountainous and inland regions. It is more common in the western half of North America.

Like the Bald Eagle, the Osprey is a fish-eater and is found near coastlines, rivers, and lakes around the world.

An Osprey near the shore of Sulton Island, Maine.

We usually think of hawks and eagles as large birds, but some of the smaller members of the family are only about the size of a robin. The tiny African Little Sparrow Hawk of South Africa measures less than 10 inches (25 cm) from head to tail. It weighs just 3 ounces (84 g) and has a wingspan of 15 1/2 inches (39 cm). The smallest North American hawk, the Sharp-shinned Hawk, is only about the size of a Blue Jay. But as a rule, hawks and eagles tend to be large. The biggest of all is the Harpy Eagle of Central and South America. It measures over 41 inches (104 cm) long, with a wingspan of nearly 6 1/2 feet (2 m). An adult female Harpy Eagle can weigh as much as 20 pounds (9 kg).

The Golden and Bald Eagles of North America are also quite large. A female Bald Eagle can have a longer wingspan than the Harpy Eagle's, but its body is smaller and lighter. As with most hawk and eagle species, the females are larger than the males.

Because hawks and eagles are predators, they are armed with strong legs and sharp, curved talons that help them kill and hold their prey. They have hooked beaks for tearing their food. At the base of their beak is an area of bare skin called the cere. The cere is sometimes brightly colored in shades of yellow and red.

Hawks and eagles hunt from the air. They rely on their eyes to locate prey, and they hunt only during the day.

Hawks and eagles can see four to eight times better than most humans. When you look up in the sky and see a high-flying hawk or eagle, you might not even be sure what kind of bird it is. But it can see you. If it could count, it could count the buttons on your shirt. A person who has very sharp vision might be called "eagle-eyed," but even the most sharp-sighted human can't see as well as a hawk or eagle. A hawk can spot the tiny movements of a feeding mouse from hundreds of yards in the air.

Eagles, ospreys, and the larger hawks known as Buteos have broad wings that help them catch warm air currents, lifting them high above the earth where they can soar for hours.

The five species of kites found in North America are smaller birds with long, pointed wings. The widespread Northern Harrier also has long wings, but with rounded tips.

The Accipiters, a group of small hawks that includes the Sharp-shinned Hawk and the Northern Goshawk, have short, rounded wings that help them chase other birds through the branches of their native woodlands.

Every hawk and eagle species has its own unique markings and colors. The adult Bald Eagle is the only eagle in North America with both a white head and white tail. The Red-tailed Hawk gets its name because its upper tail feathers are reddish-brown. No other North American member of the family has this particular mark. The Osprey is also easy to identify. This large bird is usually seen flying above water. It has a white head and belly, a dark brown stripe leading from the eye to the back, and each of its long wings has a dark patch on its underside.

But many hawks and eagles can be hard to tell apart. Sharp-shinned and Cooper's Hawks are almost identical, except that the Cooper's Hawk is larger and has a slightly longer tail. When a hawk is flying, or perched high in a tree, it's almost impossible to tell how big it is. When identifying hawks and eagles it is important to look at every detail, from the colors of the feathers to the shape of the wings and tails. Even the experts are sometimes fooled.

Young hawks and eagles are even more difficult to identify. Before they grow their adult plumage, the immature birds look more alike than ever. Immature Bald Eagles look like immature Golden Eagles. Their mottled and varied coloring makes them easy to confuse with large hawks, ospreys, and even vultures. The Bald Eagle does not get its distinctive white head and tail until it is four or five years old.

Bald Eagle landing on its perch in Alaska.

Hawks and eagles are mainly meat-eaters. They hunt other creatures, from insects to reptiles to small mammals. They hunt and kill with ease, often by surprise, coming out of nowhere to descend upon their prey. They are fast, quiet, and powerful hunters. Strong legs with sharp talons seize prey with such force that the victim dies immediately.

Some species have adapted to capturing certain types of prey.

Other species, such as the Osprey and the Bald Eagle, feed mainly on fish. The Osprey will spot a fish from high in the air and dive straight down into the water to capture it. It has spiny foot pads to help it grab and hold onto slippery fish. Bald Eagles will snatch fish from the surface of the water. They also feed on dead fish and animals.

The Snail Kite eats mainly apple snails, a large snail found in the Florida Everglades. Sharp-shinned and Cooper's Hawks eat small birds. They take their catch to a favorite "plucking post," where they pull off all its feathers before tearing it to bits and eating it.

While some hawks and eagles look for certain foods, many can and will adapt to whatever is available. The Red-tailed Hawk dines on everything from rabbits and mice to lizards, snakes, and crabs. The Mississippi Kite mostly eats insects such as grasshoppers, dragonflies, and beetles, but it will also eat frogs and small lizards. The American Swallow-tailed Kite has been known to eat everything from mice to insects to fruit!

Like other birds of prey, hawks and eagles when feeding will mantle, or cover, food with their wings in order to hide it from a hungry neighbor. These birds don't like to share territory, let alone dinner.

Different hawks and eagles are built for different styles of flying. The smaller hawks and kites are rapid, agile flyers. They need speed and quick reactions to catch their prey. Sharp-shinned and Cooper's Hawks have short, rounded wings that help them dart in and out of tree branches. The Northern Harrier takes off from low perches, flying low over fields and wetlands, ready to drop on its prey in an instant.

Eagles and the larger hawks are adapted to soaring. They hunt from high above the ground. These larger birds do not waste energy by flapping their wings when they don't have to. They seek out rising columns of warm air called thermals. They catch the rising air with their large, broad wings. The thermals carry them thousands of feet into the air in a slow spiral. You can watch a Bald Eagle soar for a very long time without ever seeing it flap a wing. Some migrating hawks and eagles use thermals during migration, coasting from one thermal to the next.

Most birds that breed in northern climates during the summer fly south for the winter. Any bird that needs fruit, fresh vegetation, or insects must travel south or they will starve. This twice-a-year journey is called migration.

Not all North American hawk and eagle species migrate. Because hawks and eagles are predators, they can survive the cold winter months. Some, like the Red-tailed Hawk and the Northern Goshawk, might fly a few hundred miles south during the winter if food is scarce, but they usually stay in the same region all year long. Many of the southern hawks and kites do not migrate at all. The Snail Kite, which eats a type of snail, never leaves Southern Florida. The Bald Eagle, a fish-eater, may travel south or to the coast to be near open water—but not always. Some eagles spend their winters in the northern United States, living on other types of prey.

Migrating hawks and kites include the Broad-winged Hawk, Swainson's Hawk, the Mississippi Kite, and the Swallow-tailed Kite. These birds all fly to South America for the winter. Swainson's Hawk is the champion migrator of the hawk and eagle clan—it flies all the way from western Canada to Argentina!

The courtship flight of the Bald Eagle is one of the most spectacular animal rituals in nature. The male and female eagles perform swooping dives, sometimes soaring together and then diving in a huge arc, down and then up again as if following the path of a giant, invisible pendulum. Sometimes the male eagle will dive down toward the female flying beneath him. Just before he reaches her, she will roll onto her back and the two great birds will clasp claws for a moment in midflight touching talons. Other hawks and eagles perform similar displays.

Most hawks and eagles mate for life. Smaller hawk species, such as the Sharp-shinned Hawk, may choose a mate when they are one year old. Larger hawks and eagles do not begin to breed until they are four or five years old. Some of the largest tropical eagles, such as the Harpy Eagle, may take as long as nine years to choose their mates.

Like most predators, hawks and eagles are extremely territorial. They don't like to share their food source with other birds of prey. During the breeding season, territory becomes more important than ever. Northern Goshawks and Swainson's Hawks have been known to attack human beings who wander too close to their nesting site.

Eagles may defend territories as large as 100 square miles (260 km^2). Smaller hawks may only need a territory the size of a few city blocks. Once hawks and eagles find a place to mate and raise a family, they may return year after year.

When human beings look for a new house, the first thing they want is a good location. Hawks and eagles also want to live in a good neighborhood. They want a home with a good view of their territory. They want to be near their food source. And they want to be safe from other predators.

When a pair of Bald Eagles search for a nesting site, they look for a location that will serve them for many years to come. Eagles need a big, sturdy tree or a rock ledge high on a cliff. Eagle nests are not your ordinary bird's nest. They don't just gather a few twigs and grasses and call it a nest. Eagles use branches and sticks, the bigger the better. They build a large, flat-topped nest large enough to hold you and several of your friends. Every year they return to the same nest and make it bigger. One famous Bald Eagle nest in Ohio sat 81 feet (25 m) above the ground in a hickory tree. It measured 8 1/2 feet (2.6 m) across, 12 feet (3.7 m) deep. It weighed about 2 tons (1,800 kg). After 35 years of use, the nest was destroyed in a windstorm.

Ospreys also reuse their nests, making them bigger every year. They like the same types of locations as the Bald Eagle, but have been known to build nests on electrical towers or telephone poles.

Of course, many nests are smaller. The Sharp-shinned Hawk builds a nest only 1 1/2 feet (45 cm) wide and 8 inches (20 cm) deep. The Northern Harrier nests on the ground, and the Snail Kite nests low in the Florida marshes, just a few feet above water.

Large eagles lay only one to three eggs, while the smaller hawks may lay three to five eggs. Eggs are laid two to five days apart. The eggs must be kept warm by the parents. This warming is called incubation. In most hawk and eagle species, both male and female take turns incubating. A few species, including Golden Eagles and Northern Goshawks, leave the incubation entirely to the mother. Incubation takes from four to nine weeks, depending on the size and type of bird.

The eggs hatch at different times. The first eggs laid are usually the first to hatch. Baby hawks and eagles come into the world wearing a layer of soft down that is later replaced by feathers. Their mother stays busy keeping each baby warm as it hatches from its shell.

While the mother stays with the nest, the father leaves to hunt for food. Growing hawks and eagles have big appetites. When the babies are older, the mother will sometimes leave them alone while she hunts for food too.

Baby hawks and eagles grow quickly. Smaller species such as the Sharp-shinned Hawk are fully feathered and ready to leave the nest in four weeks. Eagles and large hawks wait a little longer to take their first flight. Young Bald Eagles remain in their nest for 10 to 13 weeks.

The whole family stays together as the youngsters gain weight and develop into strong hunters and flyers. Even after they learn to hunt, they may still get some food from their parents. Young eagles may be fed by their parents for as long as a year.

Hawks and eagles are fierce, powerful predators, but even the biggest and fastest creatures have enemies in nature. Hawk and eagle eggs can be stolen by raccoons and other tree-dwellers. Nestlings can be killed by other birds of prey. Small hawks are hunted by larger hawks. And when prey animals are in short supply, even the best hunters sometimes die from starvation. These are dangers that hawks and eagles have faced for millions of years.

In this century, however, the greatest danger to birds of every variety comes from people. Hawks and eagles are killed by landing on high-voltage power lines. Pesticides and pollution are especially harmful to the larger birds of prey. In the 1960s, an insecticide called DDT caused large hawks and eagles to lay eggs with shells so thin they crumbled. DDT poisoning became so bad that the Bald Eagle, the national symbol of the United States, was driven to the verge of extinction in the eastern part of the country.

In the past, hawks and eagles were commonly shot, poisoned, and trapped. Farmers, hunters, and ranchers believed that these birds hunted poultry, game birds, songbirds, and livestock. There are stories of eagles stealing sheep and other livestock, and even carrying off small children, but we know now that these stories are not true. A full grown eagle can lift only about 7 pounds (3.2 kg). It is true that a few domestic and game birds are taken by hawks, but hawks also do more good than harm by preying upon rats, mice, and insects that cause crop damage.

Loss of habitat and damage to the environment still threaten many hawk and eagle species. Some, such as the American Swallow-tailed Kite and the Snail Kite, are now only seen in a small part of their former range. But for many species, the news is encouraging.

Hawks and eagles are now protected by law in the United States and Canada. Since DDT was banned in the 1970s, the numbers of Bald Eagles and Ospreys have been increasing. They are now seen across most of North America. Golden Eagles, Red-tailed Hawks, and Northern Harriers are also common in their ranges.

Nature has a way of finding its own balance. These magnificent birds of prey play a unique and important role. As long as we can preserve our woodlands, prairies, and wetlands, hawks and eagles and their relatives will soar high above us, patrolling the skies.

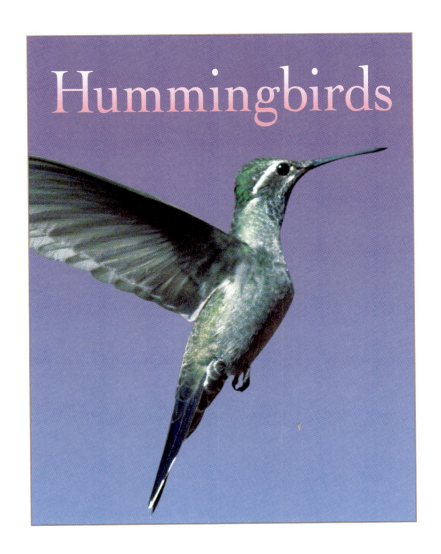

Hummingbirds

hen European explorers arrived in America, they found many strange new plants and animals. They saw herds of thundering bison, trees that seemed to reach the clouds, and flocks of birds filled the sky.

Wherever they turned they saw something new.

One tiny creature, no larger than a man's thumb, amazed and enchanted them all. It flashed red and green and purple and blue, appearing and disappearing in a colorful blur. It flew up and down and backward and forward with a strange humming sound. It could hover in midair, its tiny wings a buzzing blur. They did not know what they were seeing. It seemed too small and fast to be a bird. Could it be some sort of moth? A fairy?

They had never before seen such a creature.

The ancient Mexicans compared the birds to the rays of the sun. The Portuguese called them "flower kissers." Today, some people call them "feathered jewels" for the way they fly and glitter in the sunlight. But most of us know them by their common name.

We call them hummingbirds.

There are 338 species of hummingbirds in the family Trochilidae. All of them live in North, Central, and South America. Most types of hummingbirds live in tropical areas, where flowers bloom all year long.

Hummingbirds can be found as far north as Alaska or as far south as the tip of South America. Only twenty-three different kinds of hummingbirds live north of Mexico, with four venturing into Canada. Hummingbirds have adapted to a variety of environments, from lush rain forest to dry desert regions.

One species, called the Giant Hummingbird, is found in the Andes Mountains as high as 15,000 feet (4570 m) above sea level. Costa's Hummingbird prefers the driest of climates and lives in the desert areas along the coast of California and in the southwestern United States. The Rufous Hummingbird can be found in meadows above the treeline in the subarctic. It is the only hummingbird to venture as far north as Alaska.

Of the 23 species known to visit the United States and Canada, 22 are found west of the Rocky Mountains, mostly in the warmer regions of Southern California and Arizona.

The Ruby-throated Hummingbird has an exclusive range. In the northern United States and Canada, it is the only hummingbird regularly found east of the Rocky Mountains. During the summer, the Ruby-throated Hummingbird is common in woodlands and gardens from Texas to Florida, throughout the midwestern and the northeastern states, and up into southern Canada.

Costa's Hummingbird perched on a branch.

The smallest of all living birds is a species of hummingbird—the Bee Hummingbird. The tiny Bee Hummingbird lives in Cuba. It is 2 1/4 inches (6 cm) long—smaller than some insects! The largest of all hummingbirds, the Giant Hummingbird of the Andes Mountains, measures about 8 1/2 inches (22 cm) from head to tail. That's almost as big as a robin.

All of the hummingbirds found in the United States and Canada are between 3 and 5 inches (8 and 13 cm) long, with wingspans of about 4 inches (10 cm). The Ruby-throated Hummingbird, our most widespread and common species, is 3 1/2 inches (9 cm) long and weighs 1/10 of an ounce (3 g), about the same as one copper penny.

You will never see a hummingbird walking or hopping. Their feet are built for perching on small twigs or branches. When a hummer needs to get from one place to another, it flies.

Hummingbirds have long bills that help them reach deep into flower blossoms. Most hummingbird bills are 1 to 2 inches (2.5 to 5 cm) long, but some hummingbirds, such as the Andean Swordbill, can have bills up to 4 inches (10 cm) in length. The long bill helps the swordbill reach into the deep flower tube of a certain type of passion flower, whose nectar is its favorite food.

Hummingbirds are remarkable flyers and great fun to watch. They can hover as though they are hanging in the air. They can easily fly backward and straight up and down. Some of the smaller birds' wings move as swiftly as 200 beats per second—much too fast for your eyes to see. Their wings beat so fast that they make a humming sound, which is why we call them "hummingbirds."

Because hummingbirds are so small, cold weather can be very dangerous to them. Their tiny bodies lose heat quickly when the temperature falls. During cold spells or chilly nights, when a hummingbird can't keep itself warm by feeding and flying, it will perch on a sheltered branch, fluff up its feathers, and go into a state of torpor. The hummer's heart beats slower, its body temperature drops, and its breathing slows. Torpor is similar to hibernation. It is the hummingbird's way of conserving energy. It might last for a day, or for only a few hours. In the morning, or when the weather warms up, the hummer slowly awakens. It absorbs heat from the sun, or creates its own heat by vibrating its wings. As soon as it has warmed up, the hummer heads for the nearest flower to feed.

Hummingbirds are often called feathered jewels, and it's easy to see why. Their feathers actually appear to sparkle and shimmer like emeralds, rubies, and amethysts. As you watch a hummingbird move, its colors may appear to change. Some of the hummer's feathers are iridescent. Like oil floating on water, they can reflect a rainbow of colors. The throat of a Ruby-throated Hummingbird might appear greenish, or bronze, or black, but when the sun hits the throat feathers just right, they blaze ruby red. Feathers that looked gold a moment ago may turn to green or blue.

In most species, the male hummers are more colorful than the females, and their colors are brightest during the mating season. Males may use their dazzling plumage to attract their mates.

Many hummers are named after the color of their feathers. The male Ruby-throat has a bronze-green back and grayish white chest and belly, but his most outstanding feature is his throat, which is a brilliant metallic red. The male Blue-throated Hummingbird, one of the largest North American hummers, has a bright blue throat and dark bluish gray tail feathers with white on the tips. The bright metallic green Berylline Hummingbird is named after the beryl, a green gemstone. The male Violet-crowned Hummingbird of Mexico has a violet-colored head with a greenish-bronze back and tail.

Even though hummingbirds are tiny, they have big appetites. That's because they fly almost constantly and their wings beat very rapidly. The heart rate of hummers is as high as 1,260 beats per minute. They burn up energy quickly, so they need to eat a lot of food. In fact, they may eat and drink more than eight times their body weight each day.

The main source of food for all hummingbirds is nectar. Nectar is a kind of thin, sweet syrup found in the blossoms of most flowers. Nectar is loaded with sugars and other nutrients. The hummers use their long bills and their even longer tongues to probe deep into the flower blossoms. They feed by moving their tongues rapidly in and out of the nectar, the way a cat drinks water from a bowl. But hummingbirds are much faster than cats—their pointed tongues lap up nectar at 13 licks per second!

The hummer's ability to hover is very important for feeding. Most nectar flowers don't offer a place to perch, and the bird must eat while hovering in midair.

Hummingbirds can be very fussy about what types of flowers they like. Some species have very long or very short beaks that make it easier to drink the nectar from certain types of blossoms. Flower color is also important. The Ruby-throated Hummingbird prefers to visit red and orange flowers, and it will often fly right past blue flowers without bothering to taste their nectar. For some reason, the color red is a big favorite of the Ruby-throat. If you are wearing a red cap in the garden, you might find a hummer buzzing around your head, wondering how to get to the nectar.

Hummingbirds also eat small insects that they find in and near flowers. Their tongues have a feathery fringe that lets them hold onto the insects.

When there are not enough flowers in bloom, some hummingbird species may feed on other plant juices. The Ruby-throated Hummingbird has a special association with a woodpecker called the Yellow-bellied Sapsucker. A sapsucker will drill hundreds of holes in a tree trunk. Sweet sap flows from the holes. The sapsucker feeds on the sap and on the insects that are attracted to it. In the early spring, when very few flower blossoms are available, Ruby-throated Hummingbirds will also feed on the sugary sap.

Because hummers must have blossoms to feed on, all hummingbirds that live and breed in the northern United States and in Canada must migrate south for the winter. Some hummers spend their winters in the southern states, but most fly farther south into Mexico or Central America, where the weather is warmer and there is an unlimited supply of nectar.

But how can such tiny birds fly such great distances? For many years, people thought that hummingbirds hitchhiked south on the backs of migrating geese. We now know that this is not true. Hummingbirds are strong fliers. They can reach speeds of up to 41 miles per hour (66 kph). As remarkable as it seems, the Ruby-throated Hummingbird makes a nonstop flight across the Gulf of Mexico, more than 500 miles (800 km), on its own tiny wings.

But the grand champion of hummingbird migration is the reddish-brown Rufous Hummingbird. It flies up to 2,500 miles every spring and fall, from Alaska all the way to Central America.

Not all hummingbird species migrate. Many tropical species, such as the Buff-bellied Hummingbird of Mexico and southern Texas, live where flowers bloom all year long. They might travel a short distance in the spring and fall, but they remain in the same general area their entire lives.

Buff-bellied Hummingbird in flight.

The male hummer begins its migration to summer habitats before the female and chooses its breeding territory immediately upon arrival. The male Ruby-throated Hummingbird usually picks a spot in a wooded area, but it may choose any place that offers lots of flowering plants, such as a garden or a park. The male will fiercely defend his territory from other males, attacking with his beak and claws if necessary. You might not think that a little hummingbird would be all that scary, but imagine how long that sharp 1-inch beak looks to a 3-inch-long hummer!

Once the female arrives, the male tries to attract her by swooping back and forth, wings buzzing, making loud, high-pitched calls. Hummingbird voices may sound like a mouse, or a squeaking wheel. They use their voices mostly during courtship, or when attacking rival hummingbirds. Sometimes the female will join the male in these aerial courtship displays.

Different hummers have different courtship flights. The Allen's Hummingbird of California does a spectacular power dive from a height of about 60 feet (18 m) and reaches a speed of about 63 miles per hour (101 kph). Just before he hits the ground, he spreads his tail feathers and pulls up, making a loud ripping sound.

After mating, the male Ruby-throated Hummingbird leaves the building of the nest to the female. She often chooses to build her nest in areas that allow her a good view of her surroundings. Hummingbirds sometimes reuse old nests, but more often than not they build new ones.

The female hummer carefully attends to all of the details of construction by herself. Using lichen, bark pieces, and fine grasses, she takes seven to ten days to build her tiny nest. The inside of the nest is lined with soft, cottony plant fibers. The outside is covered with bits of lichen and bark held in place with strands of spiderweb.

Many different types of trees can be selected to hold the new nest, but Ruby-throated Hummingbirds prefer those with lichen-covered bark because it will camouflage the nest. The finished nest, about the size of a walnut, looks just like another small knot on the branch.

When the nest is finished, the female lays two tiny white eggs about 1/2 inch (1.3 cm) long. That's about the size of a small jellybean. The female sits on her eggs for 15 to 16 days. Her body heat keeps the eggs nice and warm so that the baby hummingbirds inside the eggs grow quickly.

The eggs and nest of the Ruby-throated Hummingbird.

Baby hummers are born blind, helpless, naked, and about the size of a bumblebee when they hatch. After a few days, pinfeathers or feather sheathes appear on the baby hummingbirds' bodies. Inside these sheathes, tiny, soft feathers are growing. Their final feathers quickly emerge from the white "pins."

Since they can't feed themselves, their mother stands on the edge of the nest to feed her babies nectar and small insects that she gathers and stores in her crop, which is a food pouch in her throat. She transfers this mixture to the babies by putting her long bill into their throats. Then she pumps the food from her crop to their stomachs.

The babies grow so rapidly that their bodies are too big for the nest after their first week. Fortunately, the hummingbird nest is designed to expand. The movement of the baby hummers stretches the spiderweb and plant fibers. The nest gets bigger and the babies keep growing.

Both babies are ready to leave the nest after three weeks. As a matter of fact, they're bulging out of it. They stand on the edge of the nest and flap their wings with vigor; they can actually lift off the nest for a few moments. Their mother may or may not be around when that first "flight" takes place. Young hummers instinctively know how to fly. As soon as their feathers are fully developed, they take off!

Many young hummers look a lot like their mothers during the first year. For example, the male Ruby-throat doesn't get his full iridescent red throat until the following spring when he has grown to full adulthood.

Two broods are often raised in a season. Sometimes nests can be destroyed by storms or squirrels, so the adult hummers just start over with mating and building a nest. A third brood may be raised if time permits.

Breeding and raising hummingbird families is very important to the survival of the species. Hummers often live for only a year or two. There are exceptions of course. A Blue-throated Hummingbird was known to have lived for 12 years in captivity, and one Planalto Hermit was known to have reached the ripe old age of 14. Captive birds do tend to live longer than birds in the wild because they simply don't face the same dangers.

Although hummers live peacefully with many songbirds, large mammals, and people, they do have enemies. For instance, domestic cats, if they get the chance, can intercept a hummer in midflight. Adult hummers may be hunted by small hawks, and the smaller hummers sometimes make a meal for a praying mantis.

On one occasion, a largemouth bass was seen to have leaped right out of the water and swallow a hummer whole. Hummers can also get caught in spider webs, window screens, and the spines of thistles. Young hummingbirds still in the nest may be attacked by squirrels or other birds.

Migration is a very dangerous time for these fragile little birds. Flying long distances uses up a lot of energy and makes hummingbirds more vulnerable to predators, disease, and changes in the weather. Storms, high winds, and sudden cold snaps kill thousands of hummers every year.

Hummingbirds need flowers, but flowers need hummingbirds too. When a hummingbird moves from one flower to another, it carries tiny bits of pollen stuck to its beak and head. The pollen is transferred from flower to flower. This makes it possible for the flowers to make seeds and create new plants. Without hummingbirds and other pollinators, many flowering plants could not survive.

Hummingbirds are common throughout the United States and southern Canada, but they are so small and fast that you might not notice them. To attract hummingbirds to your home, you can hang a special hummingbird feeder filled with sugar water. Better yet, you can plant lots of flowers such as hollyhocks, columbine, and petunias. Hummers prefer the red and orange varieties. A well-tended flower garden will attract plenty of hummers, and you'll also get lots of butterflies.

Whether you call them feathered jewels, flower kissers, or just plain hummingbirds, watching these amazing birds buzz from flower to flower is a wonderful summer pastime.

Loons

Sixty-five million years ago, while dinosaurs still roamed the earth, a long-bodied bird with a pointed-toothed bill and webbed feet swam through an ancient sea.

We do not know the color of that ancient bird's feathers, or the sound of its cry, but early fossils give us its shape and its size.

It looked similar to a giant loon.

Loons are the oldest family of birds on earth. No other living bird family has survived for so long with so few changes. Early North American Indians such as the Algonquin, Ojibwa, and Cree, believed that loons had magical powers. Today the loon continues to fascinate us.

When you see a loon, it is as if you are seeing into the past.

There are five species of loons. All are known for their striking appearance and mournful voices: the Red-throated Loon, the Arctic Loon, the Pacific Loon, the Yellow-billed Loon, and the Common Loon. All five species are found in North America.

The Red-throated Loon is the most widely distributed species, spending its summers in the treeless areas of northern Canada, Alaska, Greenland, and Eurasia. In the winter, the Red-throated Loon can be found along the east and west coasts of North America, and occasionally on the Great Lakes.

The Pacific Loon and the Yellow-billed Loon spend their summers in northern Canada and Alaska, and winter along the west coast as far south as the Baja Peninsula. The Arctic Loon is found in Eurasia and western Alaska.

The Common Loon is seen on lakes all across Canada and the northern United States during the summer months. They are also found as far east as Scotland. In the winter, the Common Loon lives along the east and west coasts of North America as far south as Florida in the east, and Mexico in the west. A few Common Loons spend their winters on the Great Lakes.

Loons live in many different parts of the northern hemisphere, but always on or next to a lake, ocean, or river. You will never see a loon walking across a cornfield, or perched in a tree. Loons are built for a life on and in the water, and that is where they spend almost their entire lives. They even sleep while floating on the water!

Red-throated Loon sitting on nest.

Why do modern loons look like their ancient ancestors? Maybe it's because their bodies are perfectly designed for their watery habitat.

Their strong, webbed feet are set far back on the body, which helps propel them through the water. Their wings are long, narrow, and powerful. In the air, their rapid beat can propel the loon to speeds of up to 100 miles per hour (160 kph). When diving underwater, their wings are used for balance and turning. The loon's streamlined body moves easily through the water or through the air. Don't expect to see loons walking on land, though. Their legs are designed for swimming, not strolling.

Most flying birds have evolved lightweight bones with air sacs. Lighter bones make flying easier. But loons have somewhat heavy bones without air sacs, like their ancestors millions of years in the past. The loon's heavier skeleton may help it dive deeper in search of food, but it also makes takeoff difficult. Watching a loon fly from the surface of a lake is a little like watching a big airplane—it takes a long runway to get it into the air.

Loons are large birds, about the size of geese. The Common Loon is 28 to 36 inches long (71 to 91 cm), with a wingspread of 58 inches (147 cm) or nearly 5 feet across. It weighs 6 1/2 to 8 1/2 pounds (3 to 4 kg).

Like many waterbirds, loons have a preen gland near their tail. They use their beaks and wings to spread oil from this gland onto their feathers. The oil helps the feathers shed water, keeping the loon's body dry and warm.

The loon's neck and head feathers are velvety and soft, but its body feathers are thick, water-resistant, and hard to the touch. Beneath the body feathers is a layer of semi-plume feathers, and next to the skin is a layer of fine down. These inner layers of feathers hold air to insulate the bird's body and make it easier for the loon to float.

In the summer the Common Loon has a black head with a greenish, iridescent tint. Its wings and parts of its back are covered with a beautiful pattern of small white squares and spots, and its neck is wrapped by a necklace of short white stripes. The loon's breast and belly are pure white. It has a sharp, straight, black bill and ruby red eyes. Red eyes are a feature shared by all loons. Male and female loons look the same, but the female is slightly smaller.

In winter, the Common Loon is less colorful. Its head and back are brownish gray, with a white throat and belly, a gray beak, and dark eyes. All loon species have similar brownish-gray and white plumage during the winter.

The Yellow-billed Loon, the largest member of the family, looks like a longer and heavier version of the Common Loon, weighing as much as 14 pounds (6.3 kg). It can be identified by its upturned yellow- or ivory-colored bill.

The smallest loon is the Red-throated Loon. It is about 25 inches long (64 cm) and weighs only 3 to 4 pounds (1.5 to 2 kg). It has a gray head with white stripes on the back of the neck and a red patch on its throat.

Arctic and Pacific Loons are very difficult to tell apart. In summer plumage, they have gray heads, backs and wings decorated with a pattern of white squares, and an iridescent green or purple patch on their throats. They were once thought to be the same species.

Loons are skillful hunters. They dive deep beneath the surface, using their powerful webbed feet to propel their streamlined bodies, searching for fish. Loons depend on their eyes to spot their dinner. They hunt during the daylight and in clear water where they can see fish from a distance. Most loons prefer to hunt from 6 to 15 feet (1.8 to 4.5 m) below the surface, but they can dive much deeper. The Common Loon can dive as deep as 240 feet (73 m) and has been seen to swim underwater for a distance of 1,640 feet (500 m). Their dives usually last less than a minute, but a loon can hold its breath for more than five minutes.

Loons burn up a lot of energy and have big appetites. They eat small catfish, perch, and other freshwater fish during the summer. In winter they feed on ocean fish such as herring, cod, and sand eels. They are also willing to sample frogs, crabs, snails, crayfish, insects, and occasionally some plants. Perhaps one of the reasons the loon family has survived for millions of years is because they are able to eat lots of different foods. If there are no herring to be had, a squid will do!

Because of their large bodies and heavy bones, loons can't just jump into the air and fly away. Only the smaller Red-throated Loon can take off from land. Other loons need a running start on the water. A Common Loon might have to go the length of four football fields—flapping its wings and running on the surface of the water—before it gets going fast enough to take off!

Once in the air, loons are strong, swift flyers. Their narrow, pointed wings beat 250 times per minute. In the air, loons do not wheel and turn and circle like some other birds. Loons seem to know exactly where they are going. The loon flies straight and fast, with its head held low, its sharp beak leading the way, and its webbed feet trailing behind.

Twice each year, all loons migrate. In the spring, they fly north and inland to the lakes where they will breed. In the fall, they fly south, toward the sea, where the waters are warmer and there are plenty of fish.

In late summer or fall, Common Loons begin their migration south. Sometimes a loon will fly alone, or they may gather in small groups of up to 15 birds. Loons may fly more than 1 1/4 miles (2 km) above the earth. It takes a hard rain or dense fog to make a loon delay its migration flight.

In the spring, the loons begin their journey back to the freshwater lakes where they were born. Because loons can't eat or take off from a frozen lake, they time their migration to follow the breakup of the ice. Male loons are one of the first waterbirds to show up in the spring.

Migrating Common Loons in Ontario.

Loons mate for life (about 15 to 30 years) or for as long as either partner lives. During the winter, the male and female loons may go their separate ways. But every spring, they return to the same territory where they made their first nest.

A loon's territory might be a whole lake, or a bay on a larger lake or river. It must be deep enough for them to escape from enemies by diving. It must be big enough to allow takeoffs and landings. And it must have a good supply of fish. A deep lake with small islands is ideal.

The male loon arrives first in the spring. If another loon has invaded its territory, it will drive off the intruder by calling out, splashing the water with its wings, or attacking. When the female arrives a few weeks later, the courtship begins.

The pair of loons swim together, often side by side, with their bills pointed straight up. They may rush around in a circle on the surface of the lake, calling back and forth to each other. Sometimes they take to the air together, still calling and flying around in circles, until they decide to land on the water together, breast first, with a great splash. These noisy courtship displays often happen at night.

Loons use several different calls. During courtship, the male calls to the female with a sound called a "yodel," that goes up and down in pitch. A single loon approaching a group often hoots, with a soft, careful one-note call.

When a mother loon searches for one of her chicks she makes a long call known as a "wail," which may also be used to contact a mate.

The most commonly heard call is the "tremolo." It sounds like a crazy person laughing. The loon's wild laughter is the reason for the expression "crazy as a loon," but the loon is not crazy—it may be warning other loons of possible danger.

The loon is also known to add a display to its wild and lonely laugh, especially if intruders come close to the nest or the chicks. The loon rushes at the intruder, rising up out of the water with its head drawn back and its bill almost touching its breast. Meanwhile, its feet beat away at the water, creating a spray that surrounds the dancing body. After that, the loon may dive, rise to the surface, and repeat the whole noisy performance. Most visitors leave the scene in a hurry.

Loons mate on the shore and choose a nest site that may be very close to the one used the year before. Most loons nest on islands, where they are safe from large predators. They also build nests on muskrat houses and on the mainland shore. Nests are always very close to the water, so that the loons can dive underwater quickly if danger threatens. Sometimes nests are built up a few feet from the shore in shallow water. A good nesting site has a view of the surrounding area, as well as protection from wind and waves.

The male and the female work together, gathering materials and preparing the nest for their future family. Nests are usually hidden in tall rushes and grasses. The nest itself is about 1 1/2 feet across and is made of rushes, grass, mud, and small twigs. Once in a while a loon pair will not bother making a nest at all, and the female will lay her eggs in a hollow on the bare ground.

Loons raise only one brood of chicks each year. But if a nest is destroyed by weather or by predators, they will sometimes build a new nest and try again!

Usually the mother lays two eggs that are about the size of pears. The eggs are brown and covered with dark brown or black spots. Taking turns sitting on the eggs, the parents incubate them for about 29 days. Their body heat helps the eggs develop.

A built-up nest of the Red-throated Loon in Canada's Northwest Territories.

The baby loons hatch one at a time, one day apart. One day there is one chick, and the next day there are two. The babies are wet when they hatch, and covered with downy plumes within cases of fine tissue. As the newborn chicks move around, the tips of the cases split and fall apart, and the new feathers dry off. Black down covers everything but their breasts, which are a soft light gray. About three hours later, the chicks look like balls of black fluff. Their eyes are wide open. They're ready for their first swim.

As soon as both babies take to the water, the loon family abandons its nest. But they are far from homeless. The loons move to a "nursery" area—a shallow, protected bay that is out of the wind. It must have plenty of small fish, and lots of hiding places in case of danger.

Two days after hatching, baby loons can dive about 1 foot (.3 m) under the surface of the water. When they are tired from all the exercise, they ride on their parents' backs, resting and staying warm and safe. After 10 to 14 days they are diving often and can swim 20 to 30 yards (18 to 27 m) underwater.

Loon chicks grow very rapidly, so they need to eat a lot. During their first week, they eat as often as 73 times in one day. You may eat breakfast, lunch and dinner, and probably a snack after school. That's four meals. Just imagine what it would be like to eat 69 more meals a day. Baby loons are always hungry, but they don't know how to get food. They are fed small fish by their parents. When they are one week old, they learn to catch a few small minnows.

As the weeks go by, the family travels farther and farther away from the nursery and the parents continue to bring food to the babies, even though they can now eat by themselves. By eight weeks the adults forage more and more for themselves, forcing the chicks to search for their own food. The chicks have grown into fledglings, which means that they have almost all of their outer feathers, and their feet are almost as big as their parents' feet.

The fledglings are ready to fly when they are 10 to 12 weeks old. As with all birds, flying is instinctive. As soon as the young loons' wings are strong enough, they take to the air. Once the loons can fly and feed themselves, they are on their own.

D A N G E R S

The most dangerous times for a loon are while it is still in its egg or when it is very young. Foxes, raccoons, skunks, mink, and other predators seek out loon nests. Even some birds such as gulls, ravens, and crows have been known to raid loon nests and eat the eggs. Baby loons are sometimes attacked from underwater by large pike or snapping turtles.

Adult loons are fast and strong, and have little to fear from predators. Dangers to adult loons mostly come from human beings. Many loons are killed by oil spills, or are caught in fishing nets. Air pollution from automobiles and factories causes acid rain, which kills the fish in many of the loon's breeding lakes. The noise and waves caused by motorboats disturbs nesting loons, sometimes causing them to desert their eggs.

Human beings have lived on Earth for millions of years.

Loons have been here ten times longer. The loon family has survived ice ages, droughts, floods, and other natural disasters. Their adaptability has helped them survive tremendous changes to our planet's surface. While other species have disappeared or changed beyond recognition, loons have remained almost the same.

When we hear the wild laughter of a loon, we hear echos of the distant past. But does the call of the loon also echo into the future?

As long as loons are given the space and the privacy to breed, and as long as there are fish in our lakes and oceans, loons will survive. They will remain a part of our natural world. Your grandchildren will hear the call of the loon 100 years from now. And in another 65 million years, who knows? Maybe we will all be gone, only remembered by the loons.

Robins

The Robin is the one

That interrupts the morn

With hurried, few,

express reports

that March is early on

-Emily Dickinson

How do we know that spring has sprung?

Some people go by their calendars, counting off the days. Others say that spring has arrived when the last snowdrift melts, or when the first green tulip leaves poke up from the frozen earth.

But for many people, the surest sign of spring is the appearance of the American Robin on lawns and in trees across North America. When we see our first robin of the season, we know that winter is truly gone. Even the robin's familiar song—*cheerup, cheerup, cheerily*—seems to welcome the change of seasons.

Most thrushes are medium-sized birds. They vary from the tiny Rufous-breasted Bush-Robin of southwest China and Tibet which is 4 1/2 inches (11 cm) long, to the Great Thrush from the mountains of Venezuela and Bolivia which is 13 inches (33 cm) long. The Bush-Robin is the same size as the familiar chickadee, and the Great Thrush is almost as long as our Common Grackle.

The American Robin is 10 inches (25 cm) long. It is the largest North American thrush. The robin legs and feet are designed for walking or hopping on level ground, or gripping a tiny branch high in a tree. Its beak is long and pointed, but not as long as a hummingbird's beak, and not as pointed as a blackbird's.

Watch closely the next time you spy a robin on your lawn. It will stand perfectly still and tilt its head to the side, the way you do when you want to hear a very soft sound. Many people say that it listens for the sound of moving worms. But the robin isn't listening. It is tipping its head so it can see better. When a worm peeks out of its hole, the robin quickly snatches it with its strong beak and gobbles it down.

Earthworms are one of the robin's favorite foods, but this bird is not a fussy diner. Like other members of the thrush family, the American Robin enjoys a wide variety of fruits, insects, and other invertebrates. Grasshoppers, beetles, ants, termites, caterpillars, spiders, or small snails—if it crawls on the ground, it might taste good to a hungry robin. Robins like fruit too—especially berries. They eat cherries, Juneberries, dogwood berries, and bayberries. If there is no other food around, robins will feed on apples or other large fruit.

American Robin feeding on worm.

Because thrushes feed on fresh fruit and insects, they cannot survive the harsh winters of the northern United States and Canada. Like most other birds that breed in the temperate regions of the world, thrushes must fly south for the winter. This twice-a-year movement—from north to south in the fall, and back again in the spring—is called migration.

Robins that live in moderate climates such as northern California or the southeastern United States might not migrate at all. But as the weather begins to turn cold in the northern regions, most American Robins begin to gather into small flocks for their journey south. They have been eating well all summer long, building up their reserves of body fat. They have a thick layer of new feathers to keep them warm. But by the time the first snowflakes fall, the robins are headed south, flying both by night and by day.

The robin is a strong flyer, but its top speed is only about 35 miles per hour (56 kph). The journey from north to south might take as long as a month. Some robins travel as far south as Central America. Others spend their winters in the southern United States and Mexico.

In late winter, robins feel the urge to return to their northern homelands, where they were born. The males leave first, flying north in February or early March, following the spring thaw. Sometimes a male robin will travel too far north, too soon. It is a sorry sight to see an early robin pecking at the frozen earth, searching for food. In this case the early bird doesn't get the worm!

But there is a good reason why the male robins want to get home as soon as possible. The sooner they can claim a territory up north, the better their chances of finding a mate.

About one month after the male robins arrive at their northern breeding grounds, they begin to sing. Their cheerful song—*cheerup, cheerup, cheerily*—is heard morning and evening, from April until midsummer.

Why do robins sing? Is it because they are happy to see warm weather again? Is it to entertain us? The fact is, male robins start singing because the female robins have begun to arrive. It is time to defend a territory and to find a mate.

The male's song contains two messages. It tells other male robins, "Stay away! This is my territory!" A robin's territory is not very large—usually only about one-third of an acre—but its boundaries are very important to the robin. Male robins attack any other male robin that crosses that line. Some male robins have been known to attack their own reflections in windows, thinking they are fending off an invader.

The robin's song is also an invitation to female robins. "Look at me! I am strong and beautiful! I have claimed this fine territory for you!" When a female robin appears, the male pursues her, sometimes performing a short ground display, until she agrees to mate with him.

Once the male and female robin mate, they search for a nest site together. Most robins build their nests in the crotches of tree branches, usually from 4 1/2 to 10 feet (1.4 to 3 m) above the ground. They also may nest on tree stumps, on ledges or windowsills, and occasionally on the ground. Robins may often choose nesting sites that give them a good view of their territory, and of approaching danger.

Other thrushes, such as the Hermit Thrush and the Veery, hide their nests on or near the ground, or at the base of bushes. Bluebirds are unusual—they are the only thrushes to nest in cavities. Many years ago, bluebirds nested in holes in trees. Today many of the available tree holes have been taken over by the aggressive European Starling. Most bluebirds now depend on handmade boxes for their nests. Bluebird boxes are now a common sight on fence poles all across the United States.

It takes a pair of robins from two to six days to build a nest. Both the male and the female gather nesting material, but the female builds the nest herself. She begins with weeds and grass. Then she gathers mud a beakful at a time and forms the nest into the shape of a cup. The grass and mud dry together, making a hard shell that looks a lot like a small cereal bowl. She lines the inside with a layer of soft fine grass, and the new home is ready.

The mother robin usually lays a clutch of three or four eggs. Each egg is oval and about an inch long. Robin eggs are famous for their beautiful color.

Usually the eggs are solid light blue, but on rare occasions they are flecked with brown spots. The next time you hear of a color called "robin's-egg blue," you'll know why.

The mother sits on the eggs for 11 to 14 days, keeping them warm and safe from harm while the father stays nearby, protecting their territory.

Baby robins hatch from their eggs blind, naked, and helpless. They have only a fine coating of down and must be kept warm at all times. The female keeps the babies covered, warming them with her body.

Robin chicks grow quickly and need to eat often. The mother and father take turns finding food. The hungry babies open wide, and the parents shove the food into their mouths. As the babies get bigger they are fed worms and larger insects.

Within two weeks, they are fully feathered and ready to leave the nest. Sometimes these fledgling robins jump out of the nest a little too soon. You might see a baby robin hopping about on the grass, unable to fly, peeping for its parents to bring it food.

Once the fledglings have left the nest, the male parent continues to feed and protect them. The female may return to the same nest to lay a new clutch of eggs. Robins may raise two or even three families a year.

Young robins will follow their father until they are able to find enough food on their own. Toward the end of the summer, the fledglings molt their speckled body feathers and grow their first winter plumage. They will fly south, like their parents, for the winter. When they return in the spring, they will be full-grown adults, ready to raise families of their own.

To an earthworm or a beetle, a hungry robin is a dangerous predator. Robins, in turn, are preyed upon by other creatures. Hawks, domestic cats, and other predators will attack and kill robins. House sparrows and starlings have been known to follow robins and steal earthworms from them. Climbing snakes will take young robins from their nest.

Migration is also a dangerous time. A snowstorm or a sudden cold snap might cause many migrating robins to die. Robins, as well as other songbirds, are threatened by people too. Feeding on a lawn that has been treated with weedkillers or pesticides can cause them to get sick and die. Some robins are killed by speeding cars, or by flying into windows.

Robins, like most small creatures, do not have very long lives. Most do not survive past their second year. But if a robin is lucky enough to avoid accidents, predators, and disease, it might live for as long as 11 years. One robin in captivity lived for 17 years!

Birds adapt to human development in a variety of ways. Many wild species avoid people and can only be found far from our cities and homes.

A few European species—pigeons, sparrows, and starlings—have adapted all too well. They are so common that some consider them pests.

The American Robin is one of the few native birds to thrive in our urban and suburban environments. In its natural environment, the robin and its relatives in the thrush family play an important role in the balance of nature. They help plant new fruit trees by eating berries and excreting the undigested seeds, and they eat millions of insects every day, helping to control harmful insect populations. Perhaps most important to us, the robin brings the beauty of nature into our parks, lawns, and gardens by singing its cheery song, strutting across the green grass, and showing off its proud orange breast.

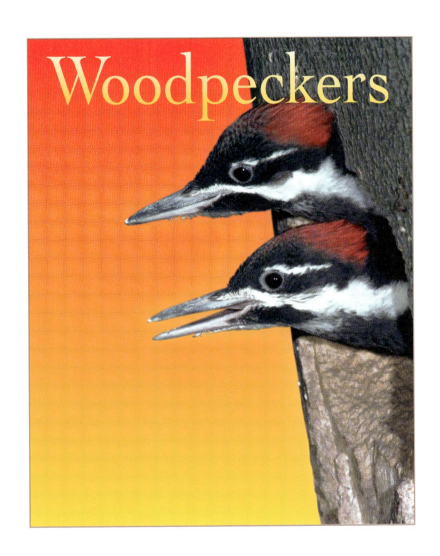

Woodpeckers

T he forest

is

never silent.

A distant honking could be traffic on a faraway freeway, or a flock of wild Canada geese. That scraping, gnawing sound could be a porcupine chewing bark, two branches rubbing together, or a proud stag polishing his antlers. The rustling noise could be a mouse foraging for seeds, a fox stalking a partridge, or only the wind on fallen leaves.

But one sound is distinctive.

When you hear a rapid hammering sound, faster than any human drummer, echoing through the trees, you've heard a woodpecker.

There are 214 species of woodpeckers in the world. Nearly everywhere trees grow, woodpeckers thrive. Only Australia, Madagascar, New Guinea, and some other smaller islands do not have woodpeckers.

In the United States and Canada, we have 21 different types of woodpeckers. From the evergreen forests of Canada to Florida's Everglades, from the towering redwoods of the northwest coast to the cactus-covered deserts of the southwest, the sound of their hammering fills the air.

Woodpeckers must have wood to peck, so most North American woodpeckers live in wooded areas. They are common in both evergreen forests and in leafy deciduous woodlands.

In tall pine and fir forests of the western United States and Canada lives the White-headed Woodpecker. The Three-toed Woodpecker is found in the spruce forests of the far north. The Black-backed Woodpecker also lives in the far north, but prefers areas that have been burned in forest fires, with many dead trees. The Red-breasted Sapsucker lives along the western coast of the United States and the pine and aspen woods of Canada.

Many other species, such as the Red-naped Sapsucker and Nuttall's Woodpecker, are found in broad-leafed or deciduous woodlands. The Acorn Woodpecker lives in oak forests where there is a good supply of acorns.

Northern Flickers, one of our most common woodpeckers, are found all over North America in gardens and parks. The Downy and Hairy Wood-peckers inhabit urban areas and are often seen on bird feeders.

The Pileated Woodpecker, the largest North American species, is found all across southern Canada and the United States, as far south as the Gulf Coast in the east and northern California in the west.

Two woodpecker species are found in the deserts of the southwest, where there are few trees. Gila and Ladder-backed Woodpeckers live in open desert areas. Instead of trees, they rely on tall cactus plants for food and shelter.

Three-toed Woodpecker building nest.

Woodpeckers come in many sizes. The Pileated Woodpecker is now the biggest woodpecker in North America, but that wasn't always true. The Imperial Woodpecker of Mexico, which recently became extinct, was 24 inches (60 cm) long—almost as big as a small goose! The common Downy Woodpecker is only about 6 3/4 inches (17 cm) long. The tiniest woodpecker of all is the Brown-capped Woodpecker of India and Malaysia, which is only as long as a ballpoint pen.

Because woodpeckers peck wood, they all have strong, sharp beaks. Because they cling to the sides of trees, they have short legs and strong feet with sharp, curved claws. Some woodpecker species have three toes and some have four. Two of the toes point forward and the other toe or toes point backward.

Woodpecker tails have two stiff, strong central feathers. The bird uses its tail as a prop when climbing or resting on the trunk of a tree. If you watch a woodpecker at work, you can see how it uses its claws and its stiff tail feathers to move easily up and down tree trunks.

The most remarkable thing about the woodpecker is its ability to peck wood. When a woodpecker pecks, it isn't just a peck here and another peck there. The woodpecker goes all out, pecking so hard and fast that its head becomes a blur. Wood chips fly every which way. It almost looks like the woodpecker is trying to hurt itself!

Of course, the woodpecker is perfectly happy banging its beak into tree trunks. It has a thick skull, a small, well-protected brain, and shock-absorbing muscles at the base of its beak. Its powerful neck muscles drive its head back and forth like a feathered jackhammer. It also has bristles lining its nostrils to filter out dust and tiny wood chips. Pecking wood is what the woodpecker does best.

Most woodpeckers are covered with black and white, or dark brown, feathers. The males of all North American species have a colorful red or yellow patch somewhere on their heads. Female woodpeckers are less showy, with more brown or gray in their plumage and less colorful heads.

The Pileated Woodpecker is one of the easiest woodpeckers to identify. This large black bird has a bright red pointed crest on its head and white patches on the underside of its wings.

The Red-headed Woodpecker is also easy to identify—it is the only one with a solid red head.

Downy and Hairy Woodpeckers are hard to tell apart until you see them together. The Hairy Woodpecker is much larger and has a longer beak.

The Black-backed and Three-toed Woodpeckers also look very similar. Both have three toes and a yellow patch on the males' heads, but the Black-backed Woodpecker has a solid black back, whereas the Three-toed Woodpecker has black and white bars down its back.

The Lewis Woodpecker has greenish black feathers on its head and neck, and a dark red face. The four species of sapsuckers all have pale yellow bellies, but the Red-cockaded Woodpecker is almost entirely black and white— only the tiniest tuft of red shows on the side of the male's head.

The Northern Flicker is covered in many colors, which vary from one region to another. Flickers are brown with black spots and bars, a whitish

rump, a spotted belly, a gray or tan-colored face, and a splash of red somewhere on the male's head. In the west, the bottoms of the flicker's wings tend to be golden or pinkish, and the face has a splash of red. In the east, the wings have a yellow underside and the red splash is on the back of the male's head.

Why do woodpeckers peck?

They peck to make holes to nest in. They peck to communicate with other woodpeckers. And they peck because they are hungry. A feeding woodpecker climbs up, down, and around the trunks of dead and decaying trees, listening carefully. When it hears the faint sounds of insects in their tunnels, the woodpecker hammers a hole with its sharp bill. It uses its tongue to probe for beetles and insect larvae.

The woodpecker's tongue is an insect's worst nightmare. It is sticky, has a barbed tip, and can reach deep into the insect's tunnels.

Sapsuckers get their name because they drill holes into living bark, letting the sap drip down the tree trunk. Insects come to feed on the sweet sap. The sapsucker eats both the sap and the insects. You can tell when a sapsucker has been feeding on a tree because it drills neat, regular rows of holes, leaving the trunk looking like a pegboard! Sapsuckers sometimes drill so many holes that a small tree might not survive.

Some woodpeckers feed on seeds, nuts, and berries. The Acorn Wood-pecker drills holes in trees and fills the holes with acorns for its winter food supply. Acorn Woodpeckers live in colonies, or groups, of three to ten birds. Since they do everything as a group, they store enough acorns to last them for several months during the late fall and winter. One sycamore tree in California was found with 20,000 acorns stuck in its trunk!

Woodpeckers fly in a swooping, undulating motion. They flap their wings and rise into the air, then glide down toward earth for a moment or two. Then it's up to the sky and down again, like a boat riding the waves. Woodpeckers usually do not fly long distances. They prefer to flit from tree to tree.

Migration is the trip that most birds make in the spring and in the fall. Birds that feed on flowers, green plants, flying insects, or fish must fly south in the winter or they will starve.

Because insects live under the bark and in the wood of trees all year round, most woodpeckers have a steady supply of food. They do not have to migrate.

One exception is the Yellow-bellied Sapsucker. Sapsuckers must have running sap to eat. Sapsuckers breed in the north during the spring and summer, but in the winter, when the sap freezes, they migrate south to Mexico and the southeastern United States.

Yellow-bellied Sapsucker at nest site.

During the winter, woodpeckers like to be by themselves. When spring arrives, they become more interested in other woodpeckers—especially ones of the opposite sex.

During courtship, woodpeckers call to one another with whinnying or rattle-like cries. The mating call of the Northern Flicker sounds like hiccups.

Woodpeckers also use their pecking ability to communicate with others of their species. They hammer on hollow trees, utility poles, metal roofs, or anything that will make a loud drumming sound—the louder the better. These woodpeckers aren't looking for food. They are looking for another woodpecker!

Different woodpecker species drum at different speeds and intervals. When a Downy Woodpecker hears another Downy Woodpecker drumming, it recognizes the rhythm of its own species.

Woodpeckers use drumming to attract mates, but they also use it to warn other woodpeckers away from their territory. Once a male and female woodpecker form a pair bond, they defend their nesting area from all intruders.

Every spring, the male woodpecker chooses a tree and starts hammering away. Sometimes the female helps with the drilling. If the tree is dead and the wood is soft, it might take only a week for the woodpecker to hammer a hole big enough for a nest. If the tree is alive, the hammering could go on for months!

Flickers, Downy Woodpeckers, and Red-bellied Woodpeckers drill their nests in dead trees. Pileated Woodpeckers and Yellow-bellied Sapsuckers prefer living trees. The Red-cockaded Woodpecker nests in living pines that have a soft, diseased center. Red-headed Woodpeckers sometimes drill new nests, but usually make do with existing holes in trees, buildings, or poles.

Woodpecker cavities, or holes, measure from 6 to 18 inches (15 to 46 cm) deep, forming a dark tunnel or cave. They are wider at the bottom where the eggs sit. Once drilling is complete, the male moves the wood chips on the floor and makes a mat that will cushion the eggs and keep them all in one place. The new home is ready.

After mating, the female usually lays a clutch, or group, of three to five eggs, but not at the same time. She'll lay one egg every day until her clutch is complete. All woodpeckers lay white eggs. Most birds that nest in dark cavities lay white eggs. Because the eggs are well-hidden, they do not need the camouflage of dark colors and speckles, and the white eggs are easier to see in the dark.

Both the male and the female sit on the eggs to keep them warm. This is called incubation. In most species, the male incubates the eggs at night, and the female incubates during the day. The heat from their bodies helps the embryos grow inside the eggs. Incubation usually takes about two weeks.

Baby woodpeckers come into the world blind, naked, and small enough to sit in a soup spoon. They are just as helpless as you were on the day you were born. Their parents take turns leaving the nest to search for insects.

The mother and father swallow insects and store them in their crops. Crops are special food storage sacks at the wide part of a bird's throat. A mother woodpecker swallows food until her crop is full. Then she returns to her nest and brings up food from her crop and gives it to the babies.

Baby woodpeckers grow very rapidly. They may eat as often as every 15 minutes. Their mother and father stay busy getting food until their youngsters can find it for themselves.

When they are ten days old, the babies' eyes are open. They hiss and cry, especially when they hear their mother or father return to the nest with something to eat. Small feathers grow in patches, and in three weeks, they're ready to climb up the wall of their home and sit at the entrance to the nest. Their parents get quite a greeting when they return!

After four weeks, or about a month, the babies aren't babies anymore. They have grown into fledglings, which means that they have nearly all of their feathers. It's time to explore the world. The fledglings perch at the entrance to the nest and flap their wings until they're in the air.

The fledglings quickly learn to drill for food. Ant hills, dead trees, and live trees become schools for survival. The young woodpeckers may follow

their parents for several weeks, begging for food, but soon they learn to find their own meals.

As soon as the young woodpeckers are on their own, the parents might raise a second brood in the same nest cavity, or they might start all over again, drilling a new nest hole.

Like all birds, the woodpecker leads a dangerous life. Hawks and owls take both young and adult woodpeckers. Squirrels and tree-climbing snakes might raid nests, stealing eggs before they hatch. Other birds, such as the European Starling, sometimes take over a woodpecker's nesting cavity before it has a chance to lay its eggs. In the northeastern United States, starlings have taken over many of the nesting sites used by Red-headed Woodpeckers. This once-common woodpecker species is now a rare sight in that part of the country.

The Red-cockaded Woodpecker has a special way of protecting its nest. This bird drills its nest cavity in living pine trees, causing sap to ooze out of the tree and around the nest hole. The sticky sap is irritating to snakes and may also discourage other predators.

Some woodpecker species are threatened by loss of habitat. Pileated Woodpeckers usually live on large tracts of old forest. When Europeans first arrived on the shores of America, they found a land covered with dense forests. During the 1700s and on into the early 1800s, trees were leveled to build homes and make room for farming.

The Pileated Woodpeckers fled to more remote areas as the forests were cleared. They had fewer and fewer places to live. Their larger relative, the Ivory-billed Woodpecker, disappeared completely and has not been seen since the 1950s.

Fortunately, many of our old forests are being preserved, and the Pileated Woodpecker has learned to adapt to younger forests and to human development.

With their red caps and distinctive hammering, woodpeckers are one of our most interesting and popular bird families. Like all creatures, woodpeckers play an important role in the forest ecosystem. They help control insect populations, and they provide shelter for other animals by drilling new tree cavities every spring.

Bird species such as Eastern Bluebirds and Wood Ducks use old woodpecker holes for their own nesting sites. Many tree-dwelling mammals, including squirrels and Pine Martens, also make their homes in holes originally drilled by woodpeckers.

The Yellow-bellied Sapsucker, by killing small trees with its drilling, helps thin out overcrowded stands of trees. It also provides food for hummingbirds in the early spring, before the wildflowers bloom. The hummingbirds feed on the sweet sap!

As long as our woodlands and forests are preserved, the drumming of woodpeckers will echo through the trees.

Bird Conservation Resources

Arizona Aviculture Society
PO Box 26899
Phoenix, AZ 85068

AST–Avicultural Society of Tucson
PO Box 41501
Tucson, AZ 85717-1501

Audubon Center of the North Woods
Box 530
Sandstone, MN 55072

Aullwood Audubon Center & Farm
1000 Aullwood Road
Dayton, OH 45414

Avian Acres
11150 Kings Valley Highway
Monmouth, OR 97361

Bobelaine Audubon Sanctuary
215 Ardmore Avenue
Roseville, CA 95678

Borestone Mountain Wildlife Sanctuary
PO Box 524
118 Union Square
Dover-Foxcroft, ME 04426

Buckley Wildlife Sanctuary
1305 Germany Road
Frankfort, KY 40601-8257

Constitution March Sanctuary
PO Box 174
Cold Spring, NY 10516

Corkscrew Swamp Sanctuary
375 Sanctuary Road West
Naples, FL 34120

Creston Valley Wildlife Management Area
Box 640
British Columbia, Canada V0B 1G0
Internet: camacdonald.com

Francis Beidler Forest Sanctuary
336 Sanctuary Road
Harleyville, SC 29448

Kaytee Avian Education Center
585 Clay Street
Chilton, WI 53014
Internet: www.kaytee.com

Lillian Annette Rowe Sanctuary
44450 Elm Island Road
Gibbon, NE 68840

Macbride Raptor Project
Washington Hall
Kirkwood Community College
6301 Kirkwood Boulevard SW
Cedar Rapids, IA 52406
Internet: ai-design.com

National Audubon Society
700 Broadway
New York, NY 10003
Internet: www.audubon.org

National Wildlife Federation
8925 Leesburg Pike
Vienna, VA 22184
Internet: www.nwf.org

Norman Bird Sanctuary
Middletown, RI 02842
Internet: oso.com/community.groups.norbird

Northern Prairie Wildlife Research Center
8711 37th Street SE
Jamestown, ND 58401
Internet: npwrc.usgs.gov

Pine Island Sanctuary
PO Box 174
Poplar Branch, NC 27965

Sabal Palm Grove Center & Sanctuary
PO Box 5052
Brownsville, TX 78523

Silver Bluff Sanctuary
4542 Silver Bluff Road
Jackson, SC 29831

Texas Partners in Flight Program
Texas Parks and Wildlife Department
4200 Smith School Road
Austin, TX 78744
Internet: www.tpwd.state.tx.us

The World Center for Birds of Prey
Velma Morrison Interpretive Center
566 West Flying Hawk Lane
Boise, ID 83709
Internet: www.peregrinefund.org

INDEX

I N D E X

I N D E X